Bundle of Deceit

Stacey Watts

Published by Stacey Watts, 2021.

BUNDLE OF DECEIT

First edition. February 25, 2021.

Written by Stacey Watts.

Also by Stacey Watts

Prologue

The bills were mounting up on Lucy Jennings' desk. She began to see that the crazy plan that she had so hastily jumped into might have been a mistake now. Life was beginning to hit her hard, and she was not sure that she had the energy anymore to fight back.

Opening the compact mirror that she took from her purse, she didn't even recognize herself. Talk about a reinvention gone bad. Of course, at the time it all seemed like a brilliant idea. It was sort of one of those crazy spurs of the moment dreams you have when life is putting pressure on you to come up with a new game plan.

Sassy Lou's Hair Emporium was her first big break into freedom. Why she just marched on in and told Miss. Sassy Lou to chop off five inches of her hair. The bob was cute but better yet; it annoyed the one man that she decided needed to be horse tied and drugged out to pasture. Walking out of Sassy Lou's gave her a great sense of empowerment for the first time in her life.

She went to her boss and marched in and told him that she no longer wanted the lying, cheating scum Kirk Dobson for her partner. She even popped her shades on top of her head like she was finally somebody. When the chief looked at her, he began to laugh. Everyone thought she was crazy, so she did what any self-respecting woman in her situation would do. She slammed her badge and credentials on the desk and walked out.

The newfound change was exhilarating. She was now ready to chart her new course.

She sold her car and most of her furniture. She bought a two-story red brick building, with the money Aunt Bertie left her when she died. She was going to become this town's best and only Private Investigator. She was going to even outshine the Sentry's Boys Club- the Sentry Police Department. The good part about this little adventure was that she could live downstairs and make the upstairs space her office.

The only thing now that she needed was a car. Checking her bank account, she realized it was close to depleted. Most people would have taken it as a sign to regroup. But oh no, not Lucy, she went right down to Harold the Junkman and bought her a car. Three hundred dollars got her a sweet little multi-colored car. Everyone needed a car with blue and yellow doors, she told herself as she sputtered away from the junk yard.

With her last twenty dollars, she placed an ad in the Morning Sentry News promoting her new business. It was a dream come true. The week was hers and nobody would ever take ownership of her life again.

Three months later, she was kicking herself. Still too proud to beg for her job back, she wondered what she was thinking. Now she had a failing business, a car that only ran forty percent of the time, and a daily war going on with the phone company.

Lucy was excited when the calls begin to roll in. To her utter dismay, they were wrong numbers. People were calling from all over town, asking her if she could locate and speak to the dead. The number used to belong to Gypsy Wanda. Apparently, she had a knack in Sentry of reaching the deceased. She often wondered if she should trade in her gun for a crystal ball. At least maybe then she could pay some bills.

Now she could blame herself for making the choices she made, but it was so much easier to blame Kirk. He was what drove her to all this change to begin with. Because after they broke up all she heard from her partner and ex-lover was *Lucy this and Lucy that,* as if he still were under the delusion that he had a right to weigh in on her life. She quickly tired of that scene.

They were no longer involved, and he was still playing confused, lonely, and *oh baby I still need you,* song on his pity violin. She knew it was only for conveniences' sake. For the life of her, she couldn't figure out why he wanted to pass down memory lane, especially when she was carrying her gun. She admitted it could be sweet sometimes, but it was not a road that she was interested in traveling down.

Her ex-best friend Arlene helped her come to that conclusion, making that little dream become a reality for her. Even now, when she thought about that day in her head, it left a sour taste that was worse than warm lemonade. The memory haunted her. It left her with many tears and heartache. Luckily, the tears turned to anger and resentment with a little side of revenge to be served up to all involved. That was the current state of mind these days. They betrayed her, and all that was left in her heart was bitterness.

She could remember the turning point that would so vividly live on as the worst day in her life. On a warm early August morning, she walked into a situation that would shake her foundation of love and devotion. In fact, after a not so stimulating night of handing out parking tickets, there would be the moment everything would change for her in an instance. She walked into her beautifully decorated town home. She walked up the stairs and opened the bedroom door. She was paralyzed and could not move. So many emotions flooded her at one time. She stood in confusion and remembered the only words muttered on Kirk the Caveman's lips. The words were simple.

"Oh Shit!"

The simple phrase with a deer in headlights looks became a nightmare. She didn't remember the clothes strewn on the floor making a trail to the bed. Just like she didn't remember Arlene Taylor wearing cheap lingerie and pleasuring Kirk in ways that she would never stoop to, with fake press on nails painted red and hooker heels strapped onto her size six feet. She just remembered the phrase that became synonymous with her entire life of sorts lately and that was clearly,

"Oh Shit!"

Chapter 1

Lila Carter closed her eyes and looked over the paper in front of her sadly, puzzled at the contents typed out in black ink. Andrew was less than two weeks old and she had never even laid eyes on him. She didn't even have a chance to give him the teddy bear she bought him.

Lila waited excitedly for her first grandson to be born. But when the time came for Early and Jenna to go to the hospital, they didn't even bother to let her know little Andrew had been born. What self-respecting son does not call his mother with good news? She wondered. Something about the whole situation was not quite right. Should she call the police? Lila read over the words again as a large knot formed in her throat.

"Would you like to order ma'am?" The pony-tailed, gum-smacking server interrupted her thoughts.

"Just a cup of coffee, please." Lila handed her the menu carefully.

"You got it, hun'!" As she hurried off to fill the order. Lila stared out the diner's foggy window trying to make sense of the cold world. She was grateful however that she wouldn't have to decide what to do about this letter. Soon Carol would be there and then maybe they could put their heads together and figure it out.

This was entirely crazy, going behind Early's back to pump his mother-in-law for information, but what else could she do? She was desperate and he was not returning her calls. The thought of them trying to raise a baby scared her a little but ultimately, she hoped it would make the wayward couple grow up some.

When Lila found out Jenna was pregnant things changed. She could not just stand back and let her grandchild suffer. Lila stepped in yet again to bail them out. She paid their rent and tried very hard to help them financially. Money was always tight, and her retirement did not go far these days. She somehow helped keep herself and them afloat and that was a miracle sometimes.

The door chimed as it opened. The chill of winter air rushed through the diner. Carol walked in. Lila motioned for her to settle in across from her in the empty booth seat.

"What will it be?" The gum-smacking server repeated her routine.

"Just coffee, please." Carol Baker said shivering in her seat.

"It's freezing out there." Carol responded as she took her seat across from her friend Lila. "Have you heard from the kids?" She asked.

"I have received a letter for Early and Jenna. I think you should read it. It accidentally arrived at my house by mistake." Lila handed the letter over to Carol.

Shock registered on Carol's face, making the wrinkles pause in time. Carol closed her eyes and shook her head in disbelief. Lila waited for her to process the words.

"Oh God Jenna, what have you done?" Carol looked at the letter carefully trying to find an answer.

"When was the last time you have heard from Jenna?" Lila asked.

"It was just about a week ago. I called to check on the baby. I was told Andrew was alright. Sleeping through the night. All the usual baby "things." I asked if I could pay them a visit and they both told me they were too busy. I just assumed they were busy being new parents and all." Lila stirred her newly creamed coffee with a spoon.

"Early has not let me see Andrew either. I tried to reason out this letter. I accidentally opened it by mistake, but it is saying what I think it is, isn't it Carol?"

"Surely Jenna and Early wouldn't have sunk this low." Carol wondered out loud.

"You are looking at thirty thousand dollars though. Those kids probably think they have amassed a fortune. Do you think they have adopted Andrew out to this Wishful Hearts Agency?" Lila asked.

"I have tried to put the thought from my mind, but I just can't seem to find any other explanation." Carol sipped on her warm coffee again as Lila stared at the letter lying on the table between them.

"I think it's time we head over there and pay them a visit." Lila shook her head nervously. Carol laid some money on the table and pulled on her wool coat.

When Lila hit the frosty night air, it sent a shiver clean down to her aching bones. Lila hurried to the car and unlocked the doors. She started and turned on the heater. Waiting for Carol to get in and fasten her seatbelt, *I wonder what excuse those kids would give her tonight,* she said to herself.

"Do you think Early, and Jenna would actually sell Andrew? The idea just seems so preposterous." Lila listened to the shock in Carol's voice as they turned the corner to Alpine Hills Trailer Court. Alpine Hills was the oldest trailer park in town. Mostly now it had become a haven for prostitutes and drug dealers. Lila had always hated going there. A few minutes' drive seemed like hours as they parked the car in the driveway.

"This is it, Carol. Time to find out what our kids are up to." Lila locked the car doors after she and Carol exited the car. Carefully, she walked up to the dark house. Knocking hard, she hoped to get their attention. The door popped open, Lila looked back at Carol carefully and with fear in her eyes.

"Early, it's mama. Are you here, son?" Lila called out into the dark room. She paused a moment and waited to see if she heard anything. Suddenly a light flashed on. She spun around and looked at Carol nervously.

"I found the light switch. No sense in us stumbling around in the dark." She watched as Carol made her way closer over to her.

Lila looked around the room. It was bare. There was no furniture. No signs that anyone was living there at all. Lila's knees went weak. Would Early really move without telling her where he was going? He was a lot of things. He was undependable, he never held down a job. He was lazy, why if she hadn't forced him to move out then he would still live down in her basement, smoking pot and not working.

She gave him credit for being a screw up, but Lila always thought that no matter what Early loved her and would never leave without a forward. Looking at the hurt and anger expression on her face, Lila could really relate to how she felt at this moment. Longing to reach out to her, she placed a warm hand on Carol's arm.

"What are you thinking?" Lila said with a compassionate sigh.

"I am thinking when I find those stupid kids. I better have not heard that they harmed or sold my grand-baby, because if they did, I may have to kill them." Lila watched as Carol fought off tears.

"I think we may need to go to the police. We have no other choice. We have to find the three of them." Both women walked carefully back to the car. A long silence cut through the chill in the air. Carol finally broke the silence.

"What are we going to tell them? Their trailer looks as though they have packed up and moved. They are adults. How are we going to prove we have anything worth looking into?" Carol said sadly.

"You know, I saw this ad in the newspaper the other day. It was a private eye. Maybe we could hire her. It seems she is deeply knowledgeable in finding people. She says her find rate is ninety percent."

"That might work out better. We can call her. Make us an appointment. We will go see her together tomorrow." Carol said.

Chapter 2

Duncan Michels watched intently as his larger-than-life boss Melinda Hartgrove breezed into the room. It must be a good day, he thought to himself. If she wore her pink dress, she was ready to flirt, and he had to be on guard. If she wore red, it meant she was some other man's problem, and she had a date later that evening. If she came in looking like a professional, that meant she was closing on an adoption. He was so glad to see her decked out in her Navy-blue striped suit. It meant he wouldn't be harassed with a lot of innuendos today.

Duncan didn't really mind the job. It was a far cry from where he worked before. The Diesel was hard on his body. It was only the hottest club in town but had its fair share of trouble. He had even worked himself up to head bouncer there. He was trained in several forms of self-defense. Security detail was a nightmare, but right out of college, it seemed the job was a perfect fit for him. The women were gorgeous, and the beer flowed freely.

However, when he reached his thirties, it was time to grow up. Duncan now remembered what his Pop's told him. "Son, go put that business degree to use." And that is what he did. Now he worked for the Wishful Hearts Adoption Agency, and he finally felt like he was helping other people. Even though Melinda could be a cougar and a drama queen, he enjoyed working there. He knew how to handle her advances and the benefits were awesome. He had a 401K, a retirement plan, and of course full medical benefits. Melinda was not stingy with her money either. She paid him very well. All he had to do was some filing and keep up with the paperwork and basic financials of the office. Well, honestly, this wasn't exactly his dream job either, but right now it paid the bills.

"Duncan, I need a file. Andrew Carter, please." Melinda spoke into the intercom system. When Duncan delivered and placed the file in front of her, she casually waved him away.

"Thank you." Melinda said as Duncan left the room.

When he reached his desk, he looked at the calendar. Jenna Carter was coming in today to relinquish her rights and give up her newborn son. Jenna never really struck him as wanting to give her baby up for adoption. She always fussed over the baby and seemed very attentive. She was not like the usual fare of girls coming in with detachment issues. Every time she spoke of Andrew, you could tell that her decision to give him up was not quite finalized in her mind.

Duncan took the Carter file and looked at it once more. So many days he had poured over the numbers, trying to figure out what was off. Something with this file was not sitting well. He had his suspicions, but there was nothing in the paperwork to hint at what he was suspecting. All the legal parts were filled out properly. All except the money. The Janny's were expecting a baby, and the agency delivered.

The problem was the money didn't add up. The standard fee was ten grand and the Janny's gave Melinda eighty-grand. He had taken the money to the bank himself. Then Melinda cut a check to the Carter's for thirty grand. Melinda walked away with a cool fifty grand. It just all seemed a little excessive to him.

He had no other proof than to sit on his thoughts and wait for more proof. The Janny's were due to come into the office at 5:30 this afternoon. He would kind of listen in to see if his suspicions were true. He was wondering if this was not Melinda taking bribes and delivering babies to the elite in Sentry.

He watched the clock tick by. When it finally reached 4:30 he heard the bell on the elevator chime. A very well-dressed man and his wife sauntered into the office. The man was balding, with a gray strip of hair combed over to the right. Duncan knew it was to hide the fact he had no hair, but it seemed forced and not natural. The wife was his age with long red nails. She walked in looking like she had stepped out of a salon. They looked like rejects from a bad reality show. Duncan plastered on a warm, smile. He knew the great District Attorney and his wife, Mr. Bob, and Mrs. Cynthia Janny.

"I will let Melinda know you are here. Please take a seat." Duncan said, motioning to the seats across the room.

"I know we are early, but we're just excited. I hope Melinda won't mind." Mrs. Janny tweeted as she sat across the room in the waiting area. Duncan walked over to the office door. Melinda sat behind her desk tapping her pen on the desk.

"Your 5:30 is here." Duncan closed the door behind him. He knew she would not be pleased.

"Damn it. I said 5:30 Duncan. They're going to ruin everything. Send them away. Tell them something." She said flippantly.

"They are waiting for their baby. What should I tell them? Maybe you should come out here and talk to them yourself." Duncan looked at her incredulously.

"Grow a pair, Duncan! Take those muscles that you tempt me with and take care of it." Melinda said with a seductive grin.

"I hardly doubt you want me to throw them out. Remember Melinda, I do have a brain beyond these green eyes you are so enchanted with." He countered back, moving inches from her lips. Duncan wished he could just once rattle her. But to no avail, Melinda sat steadfast in her chair and barely moved a muscle.

"If you are going to work for me, you are going to have to do as I say. I am in charge. Do I make myself clear? Tell them they must follow my rules or no baby." Melinda hissed. "Tell them to come back at 5:30 or else they forfeit. I very well can't have Mrs. Carter's identity compromised. They know the rules." Melinda shooed him away with a wave of her gaudy ringed hand.

"Alright, I will send them home for a while, but next time you handle your own dirty work." Duncan closed the door before she could have the last word.

"Mr. and Mrs. Janny, I'm afraid I have to ask you to leave. Melinda says you are too early. The baby hasn't even arrived yet. As per the agreement you made, it states you must follow the rules. Andrew's biological parents wish to remain anonymous." Duncan slid his glasses off the bridge of his nose.

"This is insane. I won't stand for this. We're only an hour early." Mr. Janny's chest puffed up. Duncan could see the veins protruding from his neck. He looked over at Melinda behind her desk and shrugged. He could tell that it displeased her as she tossed her pencil on the desk and stood up, giving him an angry glare. She squared her shoulders and made way to her office door.

"Bob and Cynthia Janny, so glad you are here." Melinda's voice rang through the air as she appeared from her opulent glass office. She glided over as if she was a supermodel.

Duncan sat down at his desk and watched her work her magical charm of persuasion on the unwitting parents to be. He almost felt sorry for them. With Melinda, they were not going to even know what hit them in a few minutes. She certainly knew how to calm panicked parents.

"Now folks, I know this baby is exciting. I just have a reputation to keep. My client is releasing her baby to me in thirty minutes, but she's the indecisive sort. If there's too much fuss, she might change her mind. You know how young girls can be. They can be a little emotional. I know we would all hate for her to get this far and then decide to keep him. Wouldn't we? This was a good decision for her and for you." Melinda said reasonably.

"We've spent a fortune and I don't see what the difference in us being here makes. It might not be a bad idea to see who his mother is." Bob Janny shifted nervously.

"Bob, don't cause waves. We will just come back, Melinda makes some very valid points. We were just excited." Cynthia Janny placed a hand on her husband's arm to calm him.

"Fine, I've never been able to argue with you, my love." Bob draped his arm around his wife lovingly.

"Listen, all will be fine. Trust me. I have more at stake here than you do. I have built a good name for myself, helping prominent people like you to reach your dreams. Just come back at 5:30 and then I will hand you your beautiful baby boy." Melinda casually walked them to the elevator.

Duncan watched as Melinda pushed the elevator button and made idle chit-chat with the soon to be parents. He looked back over his paperwork, hoping that he had completed all his tasks for the day. When the Janny's were on their way down the elevator, he saw Melinda approach his desk.

"Duncan, if that ever happens again, please darling, handle it yourself! That is what I pay you for. I have far too much to handle without having to deal with The Janny's." Duncan watched as she sashayed back to her large marble desk.

Jenna Carter came into the office. Her arms were empty. Duncan looked into her sad eyes.

"Mrs. Carter, may I help you?" Duncan asked softly.

"Yeah, I need to see Melinda immediately." She said nervously.

Duncan called Melinda and watched her rise from her desk and come to the door. She opened the door and smiled calmly.

"Jenna, you made it, I was about to worry. Where is Andrew ?" Melinda said cheerfully. Duncan could almost see the dollar signs dancing in her eyes. He listened carefully.

"Melinda, I have changed my mind. I do not want to sell my baby." Jenna cried.

"You made a deal. Besides, you are not selling him this is a legal adoption." Melinda said. Duncan watched her reason with a visibly upset Jenna.

"Early says we need more money. This is not quite enough. We love our baby, but we want to make sure whoever takes him will give him a suitable home." Jenna wiped the tears escaping from her eyes.

"Come Jenna, let's take this up in my office privately. I really want what is best for you." Jenna followed Melinda into her office.

"Duncan, hold my calls." Melinda called out from her doorway before she closed it. Duncan would have given anything to be a fly on the wall at that moment. He could hear the muffled voices raised.

A few moments later Jenna left the office visibly upset and shaken. Melinda wandered out behind her. She had a look of confusion and desperation plastered on her face. Duncan couldn't believe though that she wasn't panicked.

"We have a minor hiccup. I need to go handle up on this problem. Jenna and Early Carter have changed their minds. Tell the Janny's nothing of this. If I'm not back by the time they arrive, just tell them I'll return soon. I've got to go do some damage control."

"Alright. Anything I can do for you?" Duncan asked carefully.

"You are so sweet to ask. Don't worry. I will be back soon." She placed her gaudy-ringed hand on Duncan's. He knew well she was always trying to get his attention. Little signs like a well-placed hand on his thigh, or touching his hand and lingering a little long.

He was no stranger to her advances, but he would never give over to them. She was in her forties and beautiful, but he could tell she was trouble. The sexual harassment by his boss, well he was a grown man and could handle Melinda's little advances. All he would do is flirt back and keep the encouragement light. When she left down the elevator, he stepped out for a little air. Jenna Carter was sitting on a bench sobbing. Approaching her carefully, he took a seat next to her.

"Are you alright?" Duncan asked.

"I just couldn't do it. I know I promised, but he's my baby. Andrew is mine." She sobbed.

"It will be okay, Jenna. You legally may change your mind." Duncan tried to soothe her by placing a hand on her arm.

"Early and I spent all the money. Will Melinda hurt me?" Jenna sniffled back with a small groan.

"Of course, not Jenna. I'll talk to her when she gets back. It'll be alright. You go get some rest." Duncan called her a cab and waited until the yellow car arrived. He reassured Jenna and handed the driver some money to take Jenna home.

Chapter 3

Melinda rang the doorbell and stood anxiously on the other side. She adjusted her suit and hoped that Skip was around. She needed the medicine and time was not on her side. Finally, the door opened, and Skip Jordan was standing in the doorway with his red curly hair tangled in a mess.

"Hello, darling!" Melinda cooed as she reached out to pull him into a long embrace.

"Melinda, what are you doing here?" Skips' voice quivered as he spoke.

"I need those drugs. You know the ones I asked you about the other night. You said I could have them." Melinda smiled sweetly.

"Yes, I have them, but the price has gone up." He snorted. She couldn't believe that the freckled-face freak was trying to manipulate her.

"Alright, let's cut to the chase. I need to hurry. I have somewhere to be." She pushed him in and slammed the door behind him. Reaching up, she quickly unbuttoned her blouse and raised her bra up over her breasts.

"Oh yes, baby." He moaned.

Skip reached out to touch the flesh. He kneaded them in his hand as if it were pizza dough. Melinda could tell when he rose to the occasion. She didn't have time for this slow-moving foreplay. She would just have to move it along. Grabbing Skip by his collar, she pushed the little twerp over to the sofa. Unbuttoning his pants and grabbing protection from her purse, she placed it on him methodically. Straddling him between her legs. She had the power to end this. She began rocking on top of him like a rider expertly placed on top of a horse.

Several quick movements and Skip was satiated. Melinda collected her clothes and dressed quickly. Placing the syringes and vials of medicine into her cooler, she left her satisfied conquest there. Melinda walked out into sun and looked at her watch impatiently. She had to hurry, she was now officially late.

The next stop was across town. Luckily for her, it only took ten minutes to get from the East side of Sentry to the West. Melinda stepped out of her expensive sports car. Looking around at the dirty, dilapidated building ahead of her, she wiped her hands on her blue skirt. With a now or never attitude she walked quickly entering the building. She ignored several homeless men leering at her as she sat out on her mission. Birds were flying frantically overhead as she walked to the nearest mattress with a teenage girl sitting on the concrete floor.

"Celia, how are you?" Melinda asked politely.

"I'm good. I think my baby is about to come soon. I can feel her moving around more." The young girl smiled gently and ran her fingers through her long blonde curly hair.

"Celia, have you thought about my offer? I know you have a pretty pesky habit to support. Drugs can be expensive." Melinda tried to reason with her.

"No, I just couldn't. I've got plans now. I've been setting goals Miss. Melinda. I haven't had no drugs in seven whole months. When my baby comes, I'm going to get a job. My caseworker is going to help me." Celia said matter-of-factly with a dreamy hope in her eyes.

Melinda rummaged around in a small cooler that was hanging off her shoulder. Taking some sterile rubber medical gloves and a syringe, she exhaled. It wasn't the way she liked to do things, but she was in a hurry. She looked at the clear liquid in the cylinder. Thank God for Skip, the pharmacy tech. She knew this relationship would come in handy. The way she saw it was Skip, *"the self proclaimed forty-year-old virgin"* would finally get laid once in his life and she then would find herself out of this emergency situation with a labor inducing drug. It was truly a "win-win" situation.

"What are you doing Melinda?" Celia's face filled with terror.

"Quiet now, Celia, it'll all be over with soon. You will not feel any pain, I promise." Melinda pushed the needle into Celia's arm quickly before the young girl had sense enough to fight her. She hated to go to these lengths but who would ever care about a homeless, pregnant sixteen-year-old runaway.

Melinda watched as Celia went immediately into labor. She had about twenty minutes to deliver the baby and get out of there before anyone caught her. Thank God things were moving along rather quickly. When the baby was born, she looked over at Celia carefully. She cut the umbilical cord and wrapped the little bundle up in a blanket. A little twinge of guilt clouded her mind.

"Celia, I'm so sorry to do this. I know you wanted to keep your baby. Trust me, I'll make sure that your baby is cared for with a loving home. Just relax. I laced the labor inducing drug with something to calm you." She watched as Celia closed her eyes and slowly took her last strangled breath.

Melinda held the baby close and headed to her car. She had to do what she had to do. Celia was out of her misery, and the Janny's would have their new baby. She placed the baby next to her in the front seat, wrapped in a blanket. If she played her cards right, she would have twenty minutes to clean up the baby, dress her cutely and pray that Bob and Cynthia would take a girl instead of a boy.

She pulled over to a roadside rest area. Holding the baby close to her breast, she went into the restroom. Pulling many paper towels from the dispenser and turning on the warm water, she washed the afterbirth and blood away.

"Look at you. All nice and clean now." Melinda spoke into the little round eyes.

The baby cried. Melinda sat on a bench outside a rest area. Food, how was she going to feed the baby now? She rocked the fussy baby for a few moments. Melinda in all the chaos forgot to grab her purse. There were no credit cards or money to buy clothing or food for the baby.

She hummed softly, wishing she had more time to think ahead as she rocked the baby slowly, trying to calm her. Think, think, think, Melinda, what can you do next? She could call Duncan, but he needed to stay there and deal with the Janny's. She had pulled out her phone and searched her address book for help. Suddenly there was a presence looming over her. Melinda did not even notice the park ranger standing beside her.

"Poor baby. You must have had an accident." Melinda swallowed hard.

"Yes, and wouldn't you know it? I forgot my diaper bag. I think her formula is not agreeing with her. She had a terrible runny diaper and now here we are I'm afraid." Melinda hoped she was playing it cool.

"I know how it is, believe me. I am a new mom myself. Stay here, I think I might have some things in my van you can have." Melinda gave a sigh of relief as she watched the woman make way to her van.

"Alright, here you are." The Park Ranger handed her a couple of diapers, some diaper wipes and fresh onesie.

"Thank you so much. Can I pay you for these things?" Melinda offered generously.

"Shoot no, Just help another first time mom sometime. We all must pull together. You have a nice day." The brown-headed woman walked away with a warm smile.

Melinda took the baby into the bathroom. She placed a diaper and snapped the onesie on her quickly. Melinda placed her back into the car. Now she had to go clean up a bigger mess.

Melinda was now officially thirty minutes late. She came to a screeching halt in her parking spot at the office and sprinted with the baby to the elevator. When the bell chimed her floor, Melinda pasted on her best smile for the eager Janny's. Duncan shook his head in confusion as the excited couple rushed her in the hallway to see the baby dressed in pink.

"Oh, look Bob, she is so precious." Cynthia cried happily.

"Yeah, but where is Andrew?" Bob demanded. Duncan was watching the events play out in front of him like an old movie.

"Well Bob, I told you sometimes the mothers get nervous and change their minds. I was in contact with a mother today who relinquished the rights of this little doll here straight from the hospital. The mother is young and can't properly care for her. I know you and Cynthia are perfect for her. She needs loving parents like you." Melinda placed the newborn baby in Cynthia's arms. Bob's scowl softened, and he began making goo-goo sounds at his new daughter.

She smiled at Duncan, who was watching her work. She could see the amusement and the awe on his face.

Chapter 4

Lucy Jennings sat at her desk. Business had been extremely slow, and she was now questioning her decision to leave the police force and open her own detective agency. She ran her fingers through her tight curly brown tresses. The numbers on the paper were not matching up, and if she did not get a good-paying customer in soon, she would have to close her doors for good.

The last ditch effort to advertise in the news was haunting her. She had several cases to follow around cheating spouses, one case to find a long-lost relative and several prank calls. Then of course the usual calls wanting Gypsy Wanda to contact the dead. All minor, but at least they were keeping the doors open.

She had a call from a couple of old ladies. They wanted her to track down their kids. Their kids probably were in hiding. All the same, she needed the money. Looking over at the clock on her desk, she tapped her pen nervously, waiting for the appointment.

When the heavy wooden door squeaked open, Lucy straightened herself behind her desk. Two silver-haired ladies made their way into the room. She stood, plastering on her best business- like smile.

"May I help you?" She said.

"We sure hope so. Someone has stolen our grandson and we want him back." The slightly younger of the two said emphatically. Lucy introduced herself to the two women named Lila and Carol. She offered them both a cup of warm coffee. Taking a yellow fresh legal pad from the top drawer of the oak desk, she made notes.

"My daughter received this letter in the mail." Lucy took the letter from Lila. She scanned over its contents as the women sat quietly.

"They gave thirty thousand dollars to your daughter and son-in-law for their baby by a Melinda Hartgrove. Now who is she?" Lucy asked carefully.

"We think she might be a baby broker. We know she runs an adoption agency called Wishful Hearts, but we don't know why she paid Early and Jenna thirty thousand dollars. Isn't that illegal? We saw a news report stating this was illegal." Lila said in a reasoned tone.

"Perhaps this thirty thousand was for hospital expenses or living arrangements. That's not unheard of. Do you know these allegations are serious? I mean, I must be careful. If it's legitimate, maybe there is a logical reason. Maybe your children gave their baby up for adoption and these are just expenses. Could they've done that and not told you?" Lucy looked at the incriminating note trying to reason out the answers.

"Jenna and Early may be a lot of things, but they would never put baby Andrew up for adoption." Lucy watched the expression of Lila and Carol's face grow in confusion. She was curious about this case, herself.

"Alright ladies. I'll take this case. Let me do some digging and maybe I can find out more about this scenario here." Lucy sighed deeply.

"We can pay. I have a nice nest egg." Carol pulled out her checkbook. "How much should I write this check for?"

"Let's be fair. I will check out some leads for you. If it turns out to be nothing, I will charge you half of my fees. How about two-fifty to get me started?" Lucy just did not feel right taking the full amount of five hundred from the two grandmas. They were concerned and she would be able to put their minds at ease and then move on. Even though she needed the money. She would never cheat them, they reminded her too much of her Aunt Bertie.

They agreed and thanked her profusely. Lucy promised to keep them up to speed. She started a new file and placed her notes and the letter in the folder. Reclining in her office chair, she wondered why Early and Jenna just didn't tell their mother the truth. If they would've been honest, those two women would have made sure their baby and them was well taken care of.

Not like her own mother. Lucy hated to think about Ethel Jennings. She would have sold her kids in a heartbeat if she could. Ethel often left Lucy alone as young as four years old so that she could have sex with one man or another. Her mother would drink and sleep with anything that moved. The best thing that ever happened to Lucy was the day Ethel dropped her off at her Aunt Bertie's house and took off, never to be heard from again.

Lucy looked at the time again. It was nearly eight o'clock. The sun had finally set and darkness was upon her. She pulled out her keys and headed for the door. Luckily, right downstairs in the basement was her nicely furnished one-bedroom apartment.

She would just take the stairs down a flight and be home. It was a great convenience to work upstairs from where she lived. Placing the key into the lock, she heard a meow. Jinx, her black cat, skittered quickly out the door. She didn't even try to catch him. Lucy knew he would come back eventually. This was their nightly routine. He was locked in the apartment since that morning.

Lucy grabbed a frozen meal from the freezer and popped it in the microwave. She set the time and turned on the television.

"Late breaking news, police have found a homeless teen's body in an abandoned building dead. Reports confirm she was pregnant. The baby is now missing. There is a county wide search. Here is a photo of a car at the scene. A late model blue sports sedan. Anyone with any tips is asked to call the hotline immediately."

Lucy shook her head sadly. This was one reason she was glad not to be a police officer anymore. These crimes were very senseless.

Chapter 5

The next morning Duncan walked into his job with questions. He was intrigued and wanted to find out where the baby girl came from. Melinda should have documents of any new pending adoptions for him to file, and there was nothing. There was no paperwork showing anything about a female baby being adopted to the Janny's.

Something was just not right and if his suspicions were confirmed, that was his boss's car on tv last night at the scene of a homicide. Should he call the police? No, he didn't have proof, and Melinda was not to be taken lightly. Her last assistant had to move out of state because he crossed Melinda too many times. He needed his job.

Still though right is right, he reasoned to himself. He picked up the phone to make the call when the bell on the elevator chimed. He placed the phone back down into the cradle. A woman in her mid-thirties stepped off the elevator. Duncan took in a deep breath, he could have sworn she was ethereal the way she carried herself with confidence. She had brown curly hair and the bluest eyes.

"Is Melinda Hartgrove here?" The woman asked casually.

"I am sorry. She usually comes in about ten." Duncan wanted to reach out and push a wayward curl that had fallen across her cheek. He restrained himself from doing it because he was a stranger in her world.

"May I help you? I am her assistant." Duncan sat up straighter, hoping he looked a little taller.

"My name is Lucy. I'm here to get some information for a couple of friends of mine. They need adoption services. I told them I would stop in and get an application." Duncan looked for a ring and relief washed over him when he did not see one. He pulled the information from the drawer in his desk and handed it to her.

"My name is Duncan." He offered a hand to her. He wanted to feel if she was as warm as she appeared. His hand melted into hers with confirmation.

"It's nice to meet you, Duncan." He felt his heart thumping wildly when she smiled at him.

"I hope you don't find me too bold and I rarely do this, but I was wondering would you care to have a drink with me sometime?" He took the risk and ask her out. When Lucy blushed, he thought she was going to decline the invitation. But surprisingly enough, she reached down and took a pen and wrote her number on a lime green sticky note.

"Sure, would love to. How about Cooper's at nine pm, tonight? That's when I get off work." Duncan could only muster to shake his head.

"Thank you. I will see you later." He stammered.

"Thanks Duncan, see you tonight." Duncan could have sworn that she sang it with her soft voice.

LUCY GOT ON THE ELEVATOR. She was not expecting a date, but as the stars aligned and fate had it, she had one all the same. Hanging out with the assistant to Melinda Hartgrove might answer the questions she needed. Besides, it didn't hurt that Duncan was cute too, in a geeky sort of way. Those glasses did nothing for his striking beautiful green eyes. His blonde hair begged to be touched. Lucy wished she could just muss it up a little just so he might look like a confirmed bad boy.

He must have spent some time at the gym, she thought to herself. The muscles seem to ripple beneath his white starched shirt when he moved. She was breathless just thinking about those muscles taut beneath her fingertips and wondering what they would feel like. She began to softly giggle at the way he asked her out. He was trying to be a tiger in pussy-cat attire. He thought he was being bold, stumbling over his words.

Don't get her wrong. She was not ready for a relationship. Far too long she had been abused by Kirk the snake. A nice little date with maybe a romp in the bedroom might be the cure she needed to move on with her life. It was the twenty-first century, and she had needs.

Then of course the most exciting part of this day was later. She wouldn't have to go home to an empty apartment. *Score one for me*, Lucy said excitedly under her breath as she marked an invisible tally mark into the air before she stepped into the bright morning sun.

DUNCAN COULDN'T BELIEVE it. He just asked a woman, he knew nothing about out on a date. Lucy was beautiful. Somehow the way her blue eyes stared into his stirred an emotion he had not felt in some time. It was a close call, he thought for sure that he had come on to strong. As luck would have it, he had a date, and that was exciting.

His thoughts fell back to reality when Melinda's high heels were clicking on the floor. He could tell that she was in a hurry. Today the noise was almost deafening.

"We need to talk." Melinda said to him with a trembling voice. "My office." She demanded.

Duncan followed her in. He sat across from her desk. Melinda took a seat across from him. He waited for her to begin.

"Duncan, I need your help. I need an alibi rather. My car was at the scene of that murder. But you must believe me, darling, I had nothing to do with it. I just went to secure a baby for the Janny's. The police were at my house last night. I went to get the paperwork from Celia. When I tried, she said she was too tired, I was supposed to go back today and tie up the loose ends." Melinda tried to stay calm. "Can you believe she had that baby in that dirty warehouse alone? She begged me to take that precious little girl. I tried to decline, but what more could I do? I needed to get the baby safely out of there. Celia begged me to be discrete and not call an ambulance. You have got to believe me." She begged.

Duncan looked at her wildly. "What is it you want me to do exactly?"

"I need you Duncan to help me do the paperwork. Just sign her name. The signatures will be different enough. If you can do that, then this nightmare can quickly be over with." Melinda was almost begging him with her hazel eyes, about to weep frantically with tears.

"You know I can't do that. It's illegal and I can go to prison." Duncan shook his head in disbelief.

"You have no other choice. I'm in a bind here. If you don't help me, you are implicated in the crime as well." Melinda said angrily.

"What do you mean, Melinda? I have done nothing wrong." Duncan argued.

"I beg to differ. Just what do you think is going to happen? Your name is right beside mine as a witness on most of my paperwork. Do you think when they dig and find out about the baby auctions and the falsified records they will not point the finger at you as well? Come on Duncan, I know you can be clueless but you know I'm right. If I go down so will you?" Melinda warned.

"You are fucking unbelievable! Did you kill Celia?" Duncan asked her point blank, hoping she would deny everything.

"I did what I had to do to save this company. Bob Janny is a District Attorney in this town. He will have my head on a platter if I did not deliver him a baby." Melinda said as she turned to look out the window.

"It's all true then? You bitch, go to hell Melinda, I will no longer cover up your crimes any longer. If that means I go down with you, then so be it." Duncan slammed the door behind her. The walls were closing in on him and he didn't know what to do.

MELINDA WONDERED IF she was at the end of her rope. She should just clear out her accounts and head for some beach in the Caribbean. She was so over this game. Tired of catering to spoiled rich clients who wanted babies and had to have them now. All their threats and temper tantrums were over-rated. At first, when the proposition came to her, she thought about it ethically. Why the hell should she care?

She spun her chair around in a complete circle in grave thought. *I should hire a lawyer*, she mumbled. *No good*, she reasoned. They were all close to uncovering the truth. She heard a noise, Thank God Duncan had come to his senses and returned to help her. She was not alone now. Hopefully, she could reason with him. Her life was at a crossroads and there in the shadows, she saw movement.

"What the hell?" she muttered under her breath. A man stepped from the shadows and was in full view of her. Now this was just all she needed. She peered at him nervously.

"What can I do for you Early?"

DUNCAN HEADED BACK to the agency. *I'm cleaning out my desk and getting the hell out of there,* he thought to himself. If he stayed one more minute longer, Melinda would surely drag him down with her. When he approached the building, he let out a deep breath. This will be the last time he would be anyone's scapegoat ever again.

Stepping into the elevator, he pushed the number three. When the doors opened, he stepped off. Noticing Melinda had left the door open to the storeroom again, he mumbled angrily under his breath.

"Melinda, can't you at least close the stupid door?" Duncan grabbed the door and swung it hard. He made his way over to Melinda's office. He stopped just inside the doorway. Leave it to Melinda to be just sitting there staring out the window dramatically.

"I am packing up my things and leaving. I quit." He was expecting her to argue with him. She sat silently and said nothing. "Do you hear me, I am quitting." Duncan walked over to the chair and spun it to face him.

Horror filled his eyes. "Oh my God!" he screamed.

Flipping open his cell phone, he called 911 immediately. She was dead. Her eyes were cold and her body was limp and lifeless. Someone had killed his boss.

When the police arrived on the scene just minutes later, all Duncan could do was pace the floor. Looking at his watch, time seemed to tick by slowly. When the investigators were through clearing the scene, Duncan grabbed a box from the storeroom and began packing his things. Now the finality of leaving was setting in.

Chapter 6

Lucy walked into the bar. There were loud noises coming from the nearby pool hall. She peeked into the crowded room and saw two local kids laying bets.

"Hey Lucy, want a piece of the action." A kid named butch called out to her as he thumped a striped ball into a corner pocket.

"Nah, Butch. You go ahead. I am going to mosey up to the bar and have me a drink. I have a meeting." She said.

Lucy looked at Paul-the bartender, serving other customers.

"Hey man, have you seen anyone looking for me?" She shouted over the noise of music and cheering college boys watching a nearby football game. She watched as Paul poured her a tall glass of beer in a mug. Placing the liquid amber in front of her, she couldn't help but notice a grin creep upon his face.

"You got a hot one tonight?" Paul asked.

"Nope, just business. Well, maybe more, but we will see." She tried to make it light.

"Lucy, you need to date more. You find a man and settle down. You are way too pretty to be hanging out in a joint like this." He ran his hand through his silver hair, she smiled at his fatherly advice.

"Paul, if I could find a man like you, I might someday. Until then, I will wander the earth as a self-proclaimed anti-romantic fool." She sipped her beer slowly.

"Kirk was an idiot. I tell him that every time he comes in. He tells me he knows. I think boy regrets putting you back in the pond. He says Arlene nags a lot." Paul poured another beer on tap.

Lucy knew Arlene was a nagger. She was best friends with her at one time. Lucy could always remember her being that way ever since she was a kid. She tried to blame it on her parents, but ultimately Arlene found out early on that you could whine and nag and some men would fall all over her. Lucy just never thought that Kirk would be that man.

Lucy sat there alone. She checked her cell phone several times for messages. Looking at the display one last time, she realized it was quarter to ten. Paul offered her another drink.

"Looks as though Prince Charming flaked out tonight, Paul." She said with a wounded smile.

"I'm sorry, Princess. Perhaps he was held up at the office or something. I don't know any man in his right mind that would leave you waiting." The bartender said with a charming smile.

"Paul, what would your wife think about you flirting with a woman half your age? Not that I mind, it is flattering. I just don't want to end up in Sentry's gossip news tomorrow." She said playfully.

"Ah! That woman of mine. You don't think she cares. If I pay her enough money to ogle the lawn man once a week. She is all good." Lucy shook her head at Paul wickedly. Suddenly there was a tap on her shoulder. She turned on her stool to see who was there.

"I am sorry I'm late. It has been one hell of a day." She watched as Duncan took an empty seat next to her and ordered a beer.

"I was thinking you got held up." Lucy said as she took a sip.

"I'm sorry. I tried to get here as quick as I could. Let's not talk about unpleasantries. I want to know more about you." His green eyes were stunning. She noticed the little flecks of gold that shimmered in them. She was staring deeply into them when he cleared his throat.

"Earth to Lucy, did I lose you." Duncan said playfully.

"Sorry. I zoned out." She shifted nervously on the barstool, hoping, and praying that she wasn't blushing at getting caught. "What would you like to know?" She asked awkwardly.

He couldn't help himself as he chuckled softly. The conversation was awkward, to say the least. It had been awhile, and he did not know what to say.

"I am bad at dating. I have not been on one in a while." He said carefully hoping that he did not come across desperate.

"Me neither. I have just gotten out of a long relationship.

"Sorry to hear that." He placed a warm hand on hers and she felt electric passion surging through her veins.

"It's fine. I am fine just ready to kick back and have a little fun." She gave him a flirty grin.

"Let's get out of here. I can barely hear you over the football game and cheering." He shouted, as he placed a hand on her back and led her to the door. The breeze was cool when they stepped into the night air.

"It has been one hell of a day. I need to find a new job tomorrow. You don't know of a place that is hiring, do you?" he asked a little lost in thought.

"What happened?" She asked.

"Melinda, my boss is dead." She watched as Duncan tried to form the words to make what he was saying a reality.

"Really, are you alright?" She placed a comforting hand on his arm.

"I am just a little rattled. Tell your friends to find a new agency. It seems as of this afternoon, we are out of business. I called the police, and they said that it was possible she committed suicide. But I am not so sure. Melinda was always too in love with herself." He reasoned.

"Who is the investigating officer?" She wondered.

"Officer Kendal. Why?" Duncan looked at her, puzzled.

"He's a good one. I used to work with him on the force." She said.

"Used to?"

"Yep." She figured now was the time to confess what she did for a living.

"Duncan, listen. I have something to tell you." She began carefully. He stopped walking and stood under a lamp post. She resisted the urge to touch his hair that was shining in the light, she still wanted to muss it up.

"Duncan, I am a Private Investigator. I was trying to get some information on your boss. It seems she was linked to several shady adoptions." She paused a moment to let the information sink in better.

"You mean. You're not a potential client's friend. That is great." He slammed his hand angrily against the outside of Baker's Pizzeria. "Unbelievable lady, I thought you agreed to go out with me because we had a connection. Not because you wanted to pump me for information on your client. What are you going to do, arrest me? I can't handle anymore crap tonight. I have been through enough." Lucy watched as he stormed off in the opposite direction.

She knew he was frightened and scared. Could she honestly blame him? Maybe when he had time to cool off, she would make contact again with him.

"THAT LADY HAS SOME nerve!" he muttered angrily to himself.

Melinda was dead and now some PI, probably with a degree printed off the computer, was trying to milk him for information. He knew her type. She was too beautiful to care about anything but herself and getting what she wanted. No way was he going to get wrapped up in another Melinda situation. He wasn't going to pursue her romantically either.

He walked casually to his apartment. It might have been a good six blocks, but the fresh night air was doing him some good. This is turning out to be a shitty night, he thought to himself. In the shadows, lurking behind him was a figure. He felt a presence that automatically made the hairs on the back of his neck stand on alert. When he turned, all he could see was a small figure shivering in the cold.

"Hey you, come here." The voice was a loud whisper. Duncan turned around and saw her. Jenna Carter stood there with sad eyes. Duncan took a few steps closer to where she was standing. She emerged from the shadows. "Is it true? Melinda is dead." Duncan watched as Jenna swiped the tears from her cheek.

"I am afraid it is Jenna. Are you alright?" Duncan asked softly.

"No, I don't know what to do. Early wanted me to give up Andrew and I just couldn't. I'm scared, Duncan. I took Andrew and ran. I'm here to reason with you for my baby's sake. Please don't turn me in." Jenna was sobbing uncontrollably.

"Turn you in for what? You, I doubt, would be capable of murder, and the money, that has nothing to do with me. I am jobless." Duncan placed a comforting hand on Jenna's back.

"I don't know what to do. Without Early I have nowhere else to go." Jenna started sobbing again.

"You have no family? No parents?" Duncan asked.

"No, my mother will hate me. I screwed up my life again with another loser. What can I do?" Duncan shook his head. He couldn't just leave her and her baby on the streets. *Should he take her to a shelter?* He looked at his watch. The only shelter in town was Father Bristol's, and he closed at ten.

It was against his better judgment, but he had no other choice. Looking around wishing this were all a poor joke and camera men would jump out and tell him the last several hours of his life was a prank, he took a deep cleansing breath.

"Where is Andrew now?" Duncan asked.

"He is over there." Jenna pointed to a dark shadow against a brick wall of a liquor store.

"Jenna, you can go home with me. I will put you up for the night so that you and Andrew will be out of the cold. But tomorrow I am taking you to the shelter. Is that clear?" Duncan said. He saw her eyes glimmer with hope. He was hoping he had not made the worst mistake in his life.

When they arrived at his apartment, he flipped on the light. Andrew was sleeping and Jenna set the carrier with the baby down carefully. She nervously shifted and Duncan could barely stand the silence.

"Jenna, you and Andrew can sleep in my room tonight. The housekeeper came in today and she always changes out the sheets on Fridays. You can make yourselves at home in there tonight. Are you hungry?" Duncan asked politely.

"Yes, sir." When she responded in a weak, timid voice, she reminded him of a child. Duncan shook his head and fumbled around the kitchen drawer for a delivery menu. He was too tired to even try to attempt cooking something. He called the local Chinese restaurant on the corner. They are the only place that would deliver at this ungodly hour, he thought to himself.

Duncan finished calling in his order when Andrew fussed. Jenna went to the kitchen and fixed the baby a fresh bottle. Duncan picked Andrew up and bounced him. He could not believe how long it took the little guy to quiet down. It was almost immediately.

"You want to feed him?" Jenna handed the bottle to Duncan. He took the bottle and tried to remember how to feed a baby. It had been a while since his niece was this little and he had fed her. With each slurp that Andrew took, his eyes grew heavy and sleepy. Placing the baby in his carrier, he went to the door to collect the food.

Chapter 7

The little light on her answering machine was blinking. Walking over to the machine, she punched the button and recognized Carol's voice. The older woman just wanted to see if Lucy had located her daughter yet. She wished her own mother would've been that worried. Why in the world that Jenna and Early would ever want new mothers? She wondered to herself. Lila and Carol were wonderful. They cared an awful lot about their children. Even so much so to spend every cent they owned to find them.

Sitting back in her chair, she closed her eyes. The only thing she could see was her mother Ethel swinging from the pole. She was an exotic dancer, drug addict and alcoholic. Those were the only things she could do right in her life. Parenting wasn't even a thought. Ethel never even missed a step in telling her she was a mistake. It was a good thing Ethel had the sense enough though to drop her off on her Aunt Bertie. At least she loved her.

Tears filled her eyes. Lucy hated the memories that seemed to pop up out of the blue. She missed her aunt. So often since her aunt died, she wished she could still talk to her. Pushing the thoughts from her mind, she realized she needed to get back to work. No more memories, she told herself. She quickly opened a file from the adoption agency. Looking over the notes, she wondered why Melinda would kill herself. Duncan seemed to think that she was murdered.

Her job though was to find Jenna and Early Carter. The two things didn't seem to be connected but Lucy had to rule them out. Everything at this point was a possibility. She couldn't help her detective mind. Everything had meaning whether it pertained to her case.

She pulled up an internet browser and typed in Melinda Hartgrove's name. Lucy stood in awe of all the town's high society socialites and the somewhat famous on her list. So many people were contributors and had adopted from the agency. The mayor, police officers, several top officials, surely nothing was wrong and it would not involve those people in anything illegal.

Rubbing her eyes, she did not realize how tired she had become. It was time to go home. She still had not had her dinner, and takeout was all she was about to muster. Walking down the stairs and putting her key into the slot, Jinx hurried passed her in the hallway when the door opened.

Lucy shrugged her shoulders and wondered where the cat was going every night. It appeared he had more of a social life than she did. Fumbling through her kitchen drawer, she let out a breath of relief when she found Mr. Fong's order menu. Calling in her order of fried rice and orange chicken, she searched frantically for the remote control. Finding it beneath the cushion of the easy chair, Lucy flipped on the news when she was through ordering her dinner.

The top news story was the suicide of Melinda Hartgrove. Her eyes widened when the lead detective somberly spoke into the camera.

"Melinda Hartgrove owner of Wishful Hearts Adoption Agency. The police are investigating a potential suicide. We will have a memorial montage at the end of the news."

Things were becoming more and more twisted. Would Jenna Carter kill Melinda? According to her digging earlier in the day, she had found out that Jenna had backed out of the adoption. If Melinda was selling babies, maybe she was threatening Jenna. The questions swirled like a vortex in her mind.

Hearing the familiar bicycle bell in her foyer, she swung open the door. She helped the old man with her takeout bag as he teetered away from his bike. Mr. Fong had to be eighty years old, and he still insisted on driving on his bike at night delivering food.

"I see still Orange Chicken for one. When you going to get a man? You need a man." He chuckled jovially with very broken English.

"I have a male cat. Jinx loves your egg rolls. Does that count?" She countered.

"A young girl like you living alone in the city needs a powerful man to protect her. I will let you meet my son." He said happily. Mr. Fong had been trying to fix his son up for years.

"Mr. Fong, I am sure your son is nice. I'm just not in the business to date anyone right now. I'm swamped with a fresh case." She explained, hoping he would let her lack of a relationship go.

"You finally got one. I'm so happy for you. I wish you many good fortunes." Mr. Fong took his leave with a polite bow and his money, as Jinx skittered back in through the door.

The cat could smell a good egg roll for miles. Especially Mr. Fong's. He purred and wrapped himself around her legs, reminding her to feed him a bite or two with a loud meowing cry.

Lucy sat down in her kitchen. She went over her notes one more time. Some questions remained. She looked at her watch. Duncan popped into her mind. He was the closest to Melinda. Even if he knew nothing, he could have been inadvertently covering up her crimes and not even knowing it.

She picked up her cell phone. Flipping quickly through the directory, she finally found Joe Proctor's number.

"Hey Joe, it is me Lucy. I need a favor. Will you find me a number for Duncan Michels?" Lucy gave her thanks and hung up. It was a good thing that she still had contacts she could use on the force. Joe would find her the number and she would call Duncan and try to reason with him to help her.

Settling back into her chair once more with her legs folded beneath her, Lucy flipped the channels until she found an old movie. A Private Eye movie was on, she stopped on the channel. This would be what she needed to clear her head. She spooned out her orange chicken and watched intently as the sexy vixen walked into the office needing the Private Eyes' assistance.

STANDING IN THE ALLEY, Early paced nervously. The street lamp flickered above him. He wondered what his wife and baby were doing. His temper got the better of him tonight. It was better if he left. Jenna should have never backed out of their deal. She was all for the money until she bonded with Andrew. With all the reasoning and the arguing, she took off on him. The little blue-eyed baby boy was not getting a dirty deal. He was doing the best thing for him. He and Jenna were not capable of raising a baby. They could barely take care of themselves.

Now, because of Jenna wanting to keep the baby, he was going to have to provide. Babies needed stuff. They needed diapers and formula. He knew this idea was insane. Getting a job might be easier, but he was not father material. He didn't care if he got caught. All he wanted to do was show Jenna once and for all that he was not a loser.

Taking the gun from his pocket, he looked across the street. Now was the time to move. Sucking in a breath of courage, he practically stomped across the street. When he arrived at the door, he lowered his ski mask over his head and entered the liquor store.

"Down on the floor!" He said sternly. The man jumped and fell to the floor. Pushing the button to release the cash register door. Early shook his head in disbelief. There were only twenty bucks in the till.

"What the hell" he muttered loudly. "Is this all the cash?" He watched as the clerk quaked nervously.

"Yes, sir. The manager took the rest of it about an hour ago. Nightly deposit." He pointed at the sign overhead. *Cashiers only have small amounts of cash on hand.*

It figured the one night he needed the money the most would be the one night fate would give him a stupid slap in the head. Early slammed his hand down frantically on the counter.

"Wow this is just my fucking night." He took the money and stuffed it in his front jean pocket. Looking at the man who was on the floor, he hated going this far.

"You stay down and count to fifty after I leave. I won't shoot you." Early waved his gun at him and backed out the door.

Chapter 8

Jenna pulled the cell phone from her purse. She wondered if her service was disconnected yet. It did not take her and Early long to run through the thirty thousand dollars that Melinda had given them for her baby. Andrew was so sweet, the way he lay so still in her arms. It made her feel all warm and fuzzy inside. A feeling she knew Early would never feel.

Flipping on her phone, the display flashed. She had thirty-six missed calls. Five from her mother frantically hunting her down, so that she could take over her life. Two from Early's mother, who thought she was a loser, and twenty-nine calls from Early, who was quickly becoming the worst thing she ever did. She turned the phone back off. Looking over at little Andrew, she smiled. Maybe she could just beg Duncan to let her stay a little longer.

STANDING IN LINE FOR coffee was annoying. Caffeine was her drug and after the night of tossing and turning and one wild dream about her slathering coconut oil on Duncan's rock hard abs, she was irritable. Stepping up to the counter finally, she ordered her double shot latte. Paying the woman, she took a seat by the window while she waited for her order to come up.

Rubbing her eyes and squinting against the light of the sun pouring through the window, she saw him. Today was her lucky day. She had that other chance and now was the time to get her foot back in the door with him.

"Well fancy me running into you, Duncan." She said as she got up from her table.

She ignored the obvious exasperation and eye roll.

"What do you want?" He asked. She looked at him with a sheepish grin.

"No worries, Duncan. I'm not here to seduce you. I just need a few minutes of your time." She took a step closer, closing the wide gap between them.

"Fine, you have me until my order is ready. Then I am going back home, buying a newspaper, and looking for another job. You know you could seduce me." He said with sarcasm oozing from his rich voice.

"Duncan, I don't want to annoy you honestly. It is just I need help. I have this case. I just need to know how to solve it. You may be the key." She said lightly.

"Look lady, I am going to say this one time and one time only. Melinda was shady. Did I know it? Yes, but I did not know how much until the day she ended up dead. Did I kill her? No. I was, however; going to quit my job. I think she had it coming to her whether or not she killed herself." Duncan paid for his drink and pastries.

The barrister handed Lucy and Duncan their orders. Lucy walked over to the chair near the window. Duncan sat down across from her.

"What is it you want from me? I know now it is not a date." He said.

"I am trying to help my clients. I thought you might would be interested in helping me." She said sweetly.

"Oh, I know women like you. Out to save the world. I would even venture to say that your lipstick matches your shoes or whatever the hell you women do." Duncan glared at her.

"Seriously, with the attitude. You know nothing about me. I am not some wimpy girl that hides behind her make-up and hair. Give me a little credit." Lucy could feel her blood boil.

"Sorry, you're right. Perhaps I need to back off. I am angry that I have to find another job. I am mad. So just ask your damn questions so that I can move on with my life." Duncan said with a deep frustrated sigh.

"Do you know Jenna and Early Carter? They were the clients. They have a son named Andrew." She asked.

"I do. Why is it you wanted to know? I am sure they did nothing wrong other than trust Melinda." Duncan shifted in his chair nervously.

"I am not working for the police or anyone else. My clients are the couple's mother. They're worried about the well-being of their grandson. It is of great importance to reach them. You would not know where they are, do you? An address, anything." She pushed her contact file forward.

"I have not heard from them and the last address for them is correct on your file as far as I know." He pushed it back across the table.

"Alright, I just thought maybe you might have some answers. Duncan, you are a nice guy. I'm sorry about the other night. I mean, I was really interested in getting to know you." She whispered.

"You have a job to do. Listen, give me your number and I will call you if I hear anything else." She handed him a business card.

"Thank you. I appreciate it. I'm stepping way out on a limb here. I rarely do this and all games aside. Would you care to have dinner with me?" She tried to sound casual, and she was not sure why her heart was beating so wildly.

"I am not so sure that is a good idea. I will contact you if I remember anything else. You do not have to suffer through a date with me." Lucy watched him as he walked out the door.

She could see two croissants silhouetted in his white paper bag with two coffees in hand. He probably met up with a booty call after her. He was keyed up after he left her last night. She knew from little experiences with Kirk that guys needed that release.

He seemed like the type of guy that would bring a woman breakfast after a night of hot, passionate sex. She swallowed hard and bit back the feelings of jealousy that seem to rise out of no where. She sipped her drink and scribbled notes on her napkin about the case.

"JENNA, I'M BACK." DUNCAN laid his keys on the kitchen bar. "I'm sorry it took me so long. We need to talk." He handed her a coffee and croissant and motioned for her to sit down.

"Duncan, I just want to tell you how sweet it was for you to let us stay here. I hope we weren't too much trouble." She said.

"Not at all. Jenna, I ran into Lucy Jennings today. She is a private investigator. Your mother hired her to find you." He said carefully.

"Oh, that meddling mother of mine, she and Lila probably hired her to bring me in. Duncan, they are no good, I tell you. They want to steal my baby from me. I just can't let them tell me what to do." She shook her head emphatically.

"Jenna it sounds like they love you and just want to know if you are okay. Will you at least talk to Lucy and just see what she has to say? Lucy will keep it confidential." He reassured her, he felt something in his gut stir with the thought of seeing Lucy again.

"What if she tells them where I'm at? I am not sure I can take that chance." Jenna paced nervously on the floor. Duncan could not help but notice that she seemed a little frantic and paranoid wringing her hands. Jenna's eyes were cold and heavy. The dark bags under them were telling. Jenna needed a fix.

"How long have you been clean?" Duncan asked softly.

"Not long about a week. It's just getting to me. I am trying to quit for Andrew." Her gaze diverted downward with shame over her condition.

"God Jenna, you need help. You can't do this alone. Let me help you." Duncan almost pleaded. He remembered one of his college buddies nearly died from being on drugs. He at least commended her for trying but hoped to hell she would stay clean.

"I'm fine. I just need some more time." Jenna's voice cracked as she tried to hide her tears from Duncan. He walked over to the window. Staring long and hard down to the street he could not just take Jenna to the shelter and let her fend for herself. This problem was turning out to be much bigger than he had hoped it would. Once more he tried to reason with her. "Maybe Lucy could help you. Think about it. Would your mama spend money to try to locate you if she didn't care? Lucy told me that both yours and Early's mama were worried sick." Duncan said carefully.

"They are only worried about Andrew." She placed her hands against her head. She said nothing for several moments. "Maybe I can't do this alone. Call this Lucy person. I will find out for myself if my mama has changed. If she has, I will talk to her. Tell Lucy though no funny business. I will only talk to her." Duncan reached for the phone. Lucy answered distracted on the third ring.

"I know where Jenna is. We will meet you at the park. Just you. Jenna is not ready to see her mama just yet." Duncan hung up the phone. Jenna went to go get ready for the park. Andrew began whimpering. Walking over to the carrier, he picked the baby up.

"Andrew, hopefully we can help you and your mama today." Putting the fussy baby on his shoulder, he patted him gently on the back. Humming softly, Duncan hoped he would eventually quiet down.

Chapter 9

Lucy walked over to a nearby park bench. She watched as the cool wind picked up the dead leaves tossing them around carelessly. Wondering how Duncan got a hold of Jenna so quickly made her a little more than just mildly curious. Two pastries this morning and coffee, and of course turning her down for dinner when they obviously had a connection. It figured, she thought to herself. Older men tended to fancy younger women.

This took the cake though. Duncan was thirty-five and Jenna was barely nineteen. She had hoped that he had better sense than that. But impulse drove most men. She knew how impulses could destroy a person. It happened with Kirk. She saw them heading across the well manicured park's lawn. She suddenly had the urge to hit him.

When they walked up, Lucy swallowed the anger that was forming a knot in her throat back.

"Good morning Duncan." Lucy said trying to be professional with an obvious air of coolness to her voice.

"Hello Lucy. I'd like for you to meet Jenna Carter." Lucy looked at the young girl that was visibly shaking nervously like a leaf.

"Jenna let's take a walk. Duncan can stay here with Andrew." Lucy watched as the girl fussed over her baby drawing the blanket up around his chin. She looked up at Duncan with fear.

"It's alright honey. Just tell her everything. Like you told me. I promise Jenna, this is the right thing to do." Lucy felt as though her suspicions were confirmed. They were lovers. What a jerk she reasoned to herself.

Jenna agreed and walked casually by her side. The two women fell in step with one another after a few moments.

"Jenna, Lila and your mother hired me to find you. Your mother is worried about you and Andrew. She received a letter about you giving Andrew up for adoption." Lucy waited for a response.

"Oh no! They must hate me." Jenna began to sob and Lucy place a comforting hand on the young girl's shoulder. She exhaled.

"They love you, they just want to make sure that you and the baby are safe. Lila of course, is also worried about Early."

"My mother has never cared about me. She was furious when I quit school and married Early. Of course, I can see now that she was right." Lucy watched as the young girl fought back tears. She could see how much pain that life had brought her.

"Jenna let me arrange a meeting with just your mom. You don't have to see Lila. It can be in a neutral place. I promise you. I will never force you out of hiding until you are ready. But let me say this, I can tell you are shaking and nervous. The dark circles under your eyes tell me you need help. I know your mother would want to help you. Don't you owe it to your baby?" Lucy tried reasoning with her. She was getting involved and caring. She hated to be so involved but this young girl reminded her so much of her own mother. Maybe she could save her and little Andrew would never have to know rejection like Lucy had.

"Alright Lucy. I will try to meet up with her." Jenna said.

"Where are you staying Jenna so that I can reach you?" Lucy felt silly asking, but she wanted to see if it confirmed her suspicions.

"Duncan's place. He has been so nice and very caring." Jenna said sweetly. *Oh I just bet*, she thought to herself. Well, he would get a piece of her mind.

Lucy smiled gently and placed an arm around Jenna. They walked silently back to where Duncan was rocking Andrew in his carrier. When they arrived back to where he was sitting, disdain began climbing up in her heart.

"I need to have a word with you Duncan, privately." Lucy scowled at him. He walked over by a nearby tree just out of earshot of where Jenna was sitting.

"I think you are a dog for what you are doing to that young girl." Lucy said icily. "You should be ashamed of yourself Duncan. That poor girl is in enough pain and taking up with her is horrible. You need to be careful." Lucy lashed out at him as he looked on incredulously.

"Excuse me. I think you have this all wrong, as if it is any of your business. Jenna found me in the street. I let her stay with me just so she and Andrew were out of the cold. The shelter was closed last night and I don't think it is the right place for her, anyway. This is where I am hoping you can reconcile her with her mother, and I can move on and find another job." She stood there in disbelief as Duncan explained on.

"I apologize, I just assumed." She leaned back against the tall oak tree. Duncan moved closer to her.

"That is the problem with all the women in my life they just assume. Melinda wanted me to cover up her lies. Jenna sees me as her protector. Honestly, you make me crazy." He moved closer to her.

"Why do I make you crazy, Duncan?" Lucy whispered.

"Because every ounce of me wants to move that soft wayward curl on your cheek and kiss you. I can't though because you are nothing but trouble." Lucy's heart was thumping wildly in her chest. She wished Duncan would just sweep her into his muscular arms, ditching those stupid Clark Kent glasses and make her believe he was her superman.

"Why am I trouble?" Lucy countered with a soft response.

"Because, you are one of those women. You are beautiful and you don't even realize how much. Frankly, you are a tease." He placed a hand on her cheek pushing stray strands of hair behind her ear. His mere touch electrified her. She longed to stop time.

"Sweet Lucy. I will help you reunite Jenna and her mother. Then I have to find employment. If you're still hung up on me when everything is over then I will take you on that date." He pulled away with a drop dead smile. She could not believe that he was so confident of himself. She wanted to tackle him right there at the park. The way he said Sweet Lucy made her tingle with excitement. She had to regain control and her composure.

"Duncan, don't bother. I am not that desperate." Lucy braced herself and pushed off the oak tree to stand upright. How dare he think he could just smile and make her all weak in the knees? He picked up on the one thing that she tried so desperately to hide the most from him, that was she wanted him badly.

Chapter 10

Returning home from the park, Lucy went to her office. She wondered why Duncan felt obligated to help Jenna. Was there a reason? No. There was no one on the earth including him that was that nice. She began going back over the case and all the missing pieces. She was not always the greatest at solving puzzles, so sitting there until night time was doing nothing for her nerves. She rubbed her head with a moan. A headache was coming on. Popping an aspirin and downing half of a bottle of water on her desk, she looked for Carol's number.

Searching through the paperwork on her desk and thinking that it must have been replaced, she saw the hot pink sticky note that she jotted it on under her desk. Crawling under there to retrieve it, she heard her door open.

What now? She wondered, pulling herself up; she wasn't expecting anyone. The man in front of her was blonde and stood about six feet. His eyes were hard but a very striking blue.

"May I help you?" She asked quickly.

"Yeah, where is my wife and baby? Lady, don't try to tell me you don't know. I am losing my fucking patience and will not wait any longer." The strong voice boomed loudly as he slammed his fists on the desk. This must be Early, she thought.

"Early, I'm not sure why you would think I knew where Jenna was. I was hired by your mother to find you both." She countered carefully. "Why don't we call your mother? I know she wants to know you are safe." Lucy could see that he was scared and lost. She was taken back on how young he truly looked. He was just like Jenna.

"You don't understand. I am not interested in finding my mother. I want my wife." Lucy watched the fear grow in his eyes. He was in a state of great unrest. Something was not quite right.

"Early listen, when I find her I will give you a call. Will you at least call your mother? Just let the poor woman know you are alright." Lucy tried to reason with him and calm him. She had spent too many years dealing with people who were angry and unstable. He made her nervous. She would have to keep the upper hand.

"Fine, I will call her. But not now. I am fixing to go to prison. I know I will. I just need to tie up some loose ends with Jenna before I go." He sunk down into the chair across from her.

"What happened?" Lucy asked softly.

"I just knocked over a liquor store. Then, with all the cosmic forces out there to screw with me, I had only been able to steal twenty bucks. It won't be long. The police will be after me. Give me her contact. I know you have it. I know she is looking for me." Early begged frantically.

"Early, did you kill Melinda Hartgrove and make it look like a suicide? I know about the adoption and the money." Lucy asked carefully.

"What the hell are you talking about, lady? I ain't never kilt' anyone." He said angrily.

Lucy watched him as he began to pace nervously. He looked nearly wounded by the accusation.

"You mean that agency lady is gone. No, that can't be. We have a deal. They will kill me." Early began to sob.

"Calm down, Early. Tell me what is going on. Let me help you." Lucy said calmly, not sure what he was talking about. "Who is going to kill you?"

"I can't raise Andrew and Jenna and I made a deal. Jenna backed out, decided she wanted to be a mother after all. I didn't want my baby to be raised with nothing. I went to tell Melinda the truth. I saw what I shouldn't have. The people that deal with Melinda are powerful in this town. I have gotten threats and now she's dead, they will kill me, I just know it. I am sorry, I got to go." Early quickly left the room.

"Wait! Early." Lucy tried to stop him. She had to find out what was going on.

Lucy wondered if he knew more than he was saying or was paranoid. He looked exhausted. She looked out the window and watched him running across the street. Horror struck her face as she saw two bright lights speeding toward Early. She screamed and ran down the stairs.

She saw the black sedan speeding away quickly. Lucy tried to catch a plate number or something, but the car was all ready too far away. She kneeled beside him, trying to get a closer look at his injuries. It was too dark. Early lay on the ground with blood trickling from his lips. Lucy dialed 911, hoping her cell phone had enough battery power to go through. She forgot to charge it today. She told the dispatch where she was and hung up the phone and waited.

Early's eyes flew open for a moment.

"Tell Jenna and my mother I love them. I am sorry. Also, the mayor's wife…" The words trailed off as Early's body went lifeless in her embrace. Tears streamed down her cheeks.

"Early, stay with me." Lucy begged and watched as the flashing lights were quickly approaching. It was too late. Nothing made sense and Milo's wife, what did she have to do with all this?

"Lucy, I need a statement." The chief shook his head at the senseless crime before him.

"Kirk, I'm not sure what is going on. I think this is linked to the Melinda Hartgrove case." Lucy said with a shaky tone to her voice.

"Did he confess to killing her? He was being looked at for motive." Kirk scribbled down some notes.

"No confession. He was looking for Jenna. I was trying to convince him to see his mother. Then he said that Melinda was powerful and something to do with the mayor's wife. Why would Sydney Harper be involved in this case?" Lucy asked.

"Probably just the ramblings of a man on drugs. Early has violated his parole. He also knocked over Boozey's Beer and Wine shop. I do not doubt that he had a hand in Melinda's death. I know that he was trying to scam Melinda out of money with a fake adoption." Kirk tried to put the pieces together.

"You didn't see him tonight. He was scared. Not the guilty scared either that you see in murderers. I thought the consensus was she offed herself." Lucy said.

"Who else would have killed her? He had motive and no alibi. He was her killer. Lucy, you worry way too much. Why don't you go home take a hot bath? Unwind. We will untangle this mess at the station." Kirk placed a hand on her shoulder. Anger flared up in her eyes. They might have once been lovers, but that did not give him the right to patronize her.

"Kirk, you're not the boss of me anymore." She shoved his hand angrily away. Stomping back into the building, she called Lila. She wanted to get to her before the police did with all their accusations. Something was not quite right. She was going to get to the bottom of it.

Flipping through her contact book, she found the number. Lila was going to be devastated. She did not want to be the bearer of bad news, but it was better coming from her than the police or some rogue reporter with none of the facts. She was still a little miffed at Kirk. What right did he have to insinuate that Early was guilty? All the evidence was still out.

The only thing left at the scene of the crime was an empty syringe stuck in Melinda's arm. There was no sign of any struggle.

She asked Lila to meet her at the office. When she agreed, she hung up and lounged in her office chair. Closing her eyes, she sighed. This kind of thing was what she hated. A death that was pointless. She remembered when her mother was killed. Of course, it was her pimp that murdered her.

When the knock on her door came almost an hour later, Lucy was still trembling. She walked over and stood face to face with Lila.

"Come in and sit down." She watched as Lila did so. "Lila, I have some bad news and I wanted to talk to you before the police contacted you." Lucy moved closer to the older woman.

"What is it? Just tell me. I am ready for anything." Lucy could hear her voice quiver in fear.

"I'm sorry, but Early was hit by a car and died." Lucy waited for the news to sink in better. Lila sobbed uncontrollably.

"No! It can't be. He was my only child." Lucy grabbed some tissues from her desk. She handed the box to Lila. Walking across the room to the water cooler, she fixed a cup of cool water and handed her the cup.

"I am sorry. I knew you might want to hear it from me before the police came. There is more. They are trying to pin a murder on him I am certain that he wasn't involved in. He came to see me tonight. He wanted to know where

Jenna was. Early was terrified. I begged him to call you and he said he would when he left here." Lucy hoped that the news would help comfort her.

"You saw him?" Lila asked with a sniffle.

"I did. I promise you I will get down to the bottom of this." Lucy said.

"Oh dear. I can't afford to pay you for any extra. Carol was the one putting up the money for this ordeal." Lila wiped the newly forming tears away.

"No need to worry. I will find the truth. That is all I am interested in anyway." Lucy made sure that Lila was calmed down enough to drive. She walked her to her car and went back to her office.

Next on her list was she needed to call Duncan. Jenna may be the next to be in grave danger. She didn't know who would run down Early. Maybe he owed someone. This simple case of lost and found was unraveling into a hellish nightmare.

Chapter 11

Duncan sat quietly with a morose expression plastered on his face. When he hung up with Lucy, he looked over at Jenna. Damn, she should be in college. She should not be having babies and mourn over a dead husband. He didn't know how to break the news to her. Still, with everything she had been through, she reminded him of a little girl.

It was a good thing Lucy was coming over to help him give her the bad news. He didn't want to be the one to rip her world apart anymore than it already had been. Jenna was in the kitchen, she was busying herself washing baby bottles and mixing up formula, oblivious to the fact that things were about to change.

The doorbell rang, and he stood up to answer it. Lucy was here. He was relieved to see her presence in his doorway.

"I need to see you in the hallway." Duncan closed the door behind him.

"Lucy, are you alright?" He could see the fear brewing in her eyes.

"I need to stay the night here. I am worried about yours and Jenna's safety." Duncan shifted his gaze down to her bag.

"We should be fine. I can keep us safe." Duncan smiled confidently.

"Cut the macho crap! This is not up for discussion. Besides, I have guns and ammo. I dare anyone try to hurt the three of you." She said.

"So you care? I was thinking you might not." Duncan smirked.

"Don't flatter yourself, Duncan. I am protecting Jenna and Andrew. They are in my client's best interest. Besides, someone needs to be here to break the news to Jenna about Early. I am not sure you can be sensitive enough for those matters." Lucy said indignantly.

"I am not an ogre. I can be nice. You need to get a grip." Duncan reached up to brush a stray hair from her cheek. "Why is it you are nervous around me?

I must invoke some feelings of passion." He loved to see her squirm. Duncan knew it was senseless flirting, but he loved to see her cheeks blush with pink for him.

"Feelings of horror. I think you need to quit deluding yourself. Are you going to let me in or should I talk to Jenna in the hallway?" She squared her shoulders back in defiance.

"Be my guest. My place is yours." Duncan made a sweeping hand gesture and opened the door.

Lucy walked into the room and dropped her bag at the end of the leather sofa. Jenna came over to her with Andrew on her hip.

"I need to talk to you, Jenna." Lucy motioned for her to take a seat.

"Is everything alright?" Jenna asked.

"Jenna, I was at the office this evening and Early came to see me. He was looking for you. When he left, he was involved in a hit-and-run accident. He died." Lucy bit back a small strangle in her throat.

Andrew cooed and fussed to be put down. Jenna's eyes teared up, and she sobbed. Duncan took Andrew, placing him gently into the nearby playpen. Lucy moved over and took Jenna into her arms. She held her there until she could gain some of her composure.

Duncan observed Lucy. She was so tough yet extremely sensitive and compassionate. Walking over to the kitchen, he felt helpless. Every emotion in his body screamed out to protect them. Who should he protect them from? He wondered. None of this made any kind of sense.

"I'm sorry, Jenna." Lucy said. "I wanted to ask you why he might be targeted."

"Early was in trouble. He was with Melinda and someone else. It had something to do with blackmail. He called me the other night and told me he wanted me back. He was trying to get enough money together so we could start over." Jenna rubbed her cheeks.

"Did he say who he was trying to blackmail?" Lucy asked.

"No, I didn't talk to him. These were all voicemails." Jenna handed Lucy the phone.

The sudden explosion of glass shattering in the front window caused Lucy to react. Instinctively, she pulled Jenna to the floor behind the sofa and shielded her with her body. Duncan ducked behind the bar. Lucy pulled her handgun from her bag. The noise startled Andrew, who was now crying.

She crawled over to the playpen carefully and pulled the baby out. Lucy handed him to Jenna. After a few moments when things seemed quiet, she walked over to the broken window. There was a brick with a note attached. The words were written in red ink.

Poor sweet little Jenna. You will be reunited with your husband soon. I will have your baby.

"What the hell happened? Duncan said from the kitchen.

"Well, it seems someone is trying to get to Jenna and the baby. You are not safe here. Pack up. We are moving." Lucy was not sure where she would go. Here was not the best place. Too many windows were a nightmare. Picking up the telephone, she called the police. Whoever threw the brick would not be bold enough to come back while the police were on the scene, she hoped.

"Duncan, take your car with Jenna and Andrew. Here is the key to my office go there and bolt the door." She gave him directions quickly. "Do not stop anywhere. I will be along as soon as I can." Duncan grabbed a bag and began throwing clothes into it.

"Should I wait for you?" Lucy looked at the fear in his eyes. He was scared. The flirtatious behavior was gone and so was the careless attitude.

"I will be along as soon as I can. I need to talk to Chief Kirk. No one needs to know Jenna's whereabouts. Let me get this sorted out. Here is my cell phone number. Call me should you need anything. Keep Jenna and the baby safe." Lucy said. She took her phone out and plugged it up to the wall. She hoped that it would charge up rather quickly.

She escorted them to the car. Helping them get Andrew strapped in, she told them to be safe. When the car took off, she saw Kirk's 4x4 truck approaching. He stepped out on the dark street.

"What do we have here?" Kirk said gruffly.

"Someone threw a brick at Melinda's assistant's window. He called me rather shaken up. He hated to leave but went to stay with his brother until things blew over." Lucy hated to lie to him. If Early was right, there was corruption and baby brokering going on as high as the mayor. There was no way while she was holding the cards, she was going to allude to anything.

"Why would anyone want to throw a brick through his window? It was probably just some kids out after a night of partying. Why is it I keep running into you whenever I am investigating this case?" Kirk looked around the room quietly. She knew he was going to have to be told.

"I was hired by Early and Jenna's mother to locate them." Lucy said quickly.

"Not that I mind your input, but you quit your job. You can come back anytime. I will assign you a new partner." Kirk said.

"No, thank you. I like my new job. It's rewarding." She said knowing full well it was all lies.

Lucy walked over to the other side of the room and peered out the broken window. She had no other choice but to send Jenna away. Perhaps Lila and Carol would take her away and find her a safe place to lie low with Andrew out of harm's way.

Lucy knew the letter was intended for Jenna. However; Duncan was becoming a target as well. People had to know that Duncan was Melinda's assistant. She hoped he could access the files in she could find out what was going on. If she could access the files, maybe she can find out if Melinda Hartgrove were dealing in selling babies.

She waited for Kirk to finish up his investigation. Before he left, he sauntered over to Lucy.

"Are you alright?" Kirk placed a hand on her cheek.

"I am fine. I am just wondering what is going on in Sentry? First Melinda, then Early and now this." She exhaled.

"Oh Lucy, I miss you so much. Arlene just can't compare to you." He whispered just mere inches from her face.

"You made your bed Kirk, you and Arlene deserve one another." She said, anger rising in her cheeks.

"How many times am I going to apologize?" He said. The other officers just kept working. They were used to the constant flying sparks between them.

"You're living with Arlene. You are crazy, Kirk. You don't know what the hell you want. You want me to just turn a blind eye when you cheat. What the hell?" She screamed.

"You know I can't stand to be lonely. I wanted you to marry me. I need you back in my life." He retorted.

"Not going to happen. Believe it or not, I am done. Besides, you were the one punishing me. I am done." She stood defiantly eying him. She wouldn't give him the satisfaction of being wounded anymore.

When he finally got into his truck and left, she locked the door to Duncan's apartment and headed back to the office. When she arrived, Duncan and Jenna were sitting in the office on the sofa. Andrew was asleep in his playpen.

"Jenna, I am calling your mom and Lila. I want the four of you to leave town until we figure this out. If you do not go, you will put your baby in harm's way." Lucy tried to be as direct as possible.

"But my mom, will be angry. Lila will blame me for Early's death." Lucy watched as Jenna placed her hands over her face and sobbed.

"It is time for you to grow up. Lila and Carol are concerned about you. They made sure that you and Andrew were all right. They want to help you. If I were you, I would take this opportunity to straighten out your life and let them help you with Andrew. I am calling them to pick you up right away." Lucy hated to be so firm with Jenna. But if this is what it took to protect her, then so be it.

Chapter 12

Lucy opened the door for Lila and Carol. She explained the situation to them and told them they needed to leave town. Carol's sister had a cabin about four hours away and they were going to take Jenna and Andrew there and stay and help with the baby. Andrew snuggled down into Lila's shoulder. Jenna took her mother's hand, and they left. Lucy was relieved when she saw both women hugging Jenna and giving her love. She knew that this was not a mistake.

Lucy leaned back in her office chair with a sigh of relief. She looked over at Duncan sitting there with a confused look on his face.

"What just happened?" he said.

"I knew that Lila and Carol would never turn their back's on Jenna. They love their grandson and they love Jenna. Jenna just needed to realize that they wouldn't hurt them. She still seeks their approval. She is very much like a child in those aspects." She said.

"I guess it's time for me to go back home. I am so glad that things worked out. If there is anything I can do, please let me know?" Lucy watched as Duncan stood up from the sofa.

"Just a minute, I do not think it's safe for you to go back there. There is still a mad person out for Jenna. They would not stop at hurting you. I would feel much better if you stayed here with me." Lucy could see the annoyance rising in his eyes.

"You want me to stay with you. Here, I am not sure that that is a good idea. I think I could take care of myself." Lucy shook her head and said fine if you feel you must go, you must go. I am trained I have weapons. You are in the safest place in town. Early said that Melinda was dealing with some top officials. I know, and you know half the town has their hands in one way or another with the Wishful Hearts Agency. Like it or not, you are a target. Those people will stop at nothing to cover up their crimes." Lucy walked over to where he was standing and placed a comforting hand on his arm.

"I am not sure what I have to do with all this. I do not even have a job. I saw nothing illegal. Just questionable. I just want to move on with my life." Lucy could tell from the frustration in his voice. She just couldn't put him in harm's way.

"I am just asking for a couple of days. I want to investigate this further. I have done my job with Lila and Carol. There are just some things that are not sitting well with me. I have some questions. I think you are in the perfect position to answer them. If in a few days things check out, I will let you go back home and you will never have to see me again. Please just humor me on this." Lucy wanted to reason with him.

"I will stay here. I'll answer your questions as best I can. I'm curious to get to the bottom of things myself. I don't like loose ends." He rubbed his cheek as he spoke.

Lucy and Duncan walked downstairs to her apartment. When she opened the door, Jinx skittered out. She walked in, flipping on lights as she went. She could not stand to be in a dark apartment, it made her feel unsafe.

"Wow, nice place. I figured you would be an organized freak." Lucy looked around her apartment and rolled her eyes at his sarcastic tone.

"What? This is clean." She walked over and put water in the kettle to boil.

"You really were a police officer. Oh, this just keeps getting better. Are you undercover or something? Should I be worried?" She watched him read her certificate from training at the police Academy.

"I used to be an officer, I worked for years on the streets. I got out of it because I didn't like the crime and seeing what it does to people. I just went into business as a private investigator. This is like police work in a much milder form, or at least it used to be." Lucy poured boiling water into two teacups. Placing a tea bag into each cup, she handed one to Duncan.

"You are just full of surprises. I just really figured you to be one of those girls who was out playing a police officer." He said.

"Duncan, I may check on extramarital affairs. I may help people find lost friends and family. That does not make me less of a person. I don't come to your job and bash what you do?

Talk about stereotypes. You would think in a position of secretary at an adoption agency that you of all people would understand." Lucy was losing her temper. Who did he think he was to question her abilities at her job? He really had some nerve.

"Touché, I apologize. Let's start over, it seems we've gotten on the wrong side of each other. Every time we get together we end up arguing. If we're going to work together on finding out who killed Melinda and Early we need to work together." Lucy watched as Duncan sipped his tea between comments. Even the way he pursed his lips taking in the hot liquid was sexy.

"I am sorry too. I am really stressed out over this case. I have tried so hard to not get involved, but I must. It's who I am, I suppose. The good news is with Jenna and Andrew safe I can focus on what's going on and see what really happened to Melinda Hartgrove? Do you have any ideas on this?" She watched this Duncan sipped his tea.

"Melinda was one of those complicated people. She knew how to put on a show. I spent most of my time cleaning up her messes and then she would still come out on top smelling like a rose. My only problem is I fear, that I am going to be implicated in her crimes. My name was on most of the documents that were signed except for the last ones."

"What were the last documents if you don't mind me asking?" Lucy pulled out her notebook and took notes.

"Well Melinda wanted me to forge a name on a document for adoption. Several days ago, a young girl named Celia Barlow was murdered. I am sure that Melinda had something to do with it. Jenna and Early was supposed to put their baby Andrew up for adoption. Jenna got scared and changed her mind. Jenna for some wild reason kept telling me that Melinda was going to harm her for spending all the money they were given." Duncan replied.

"So that is where the $30,000 came into play. What happened next?" Lucy asked jotting down some notes in her notebook.

"Well Jenna left. I had a falling out with Melinda about her car being placed at the scene. She said the car was hers, but that Celia Barlow placed her baby up for adoption. She tried to convince me, she was just too tired to sign the papers. She wanted me to falsify them and sign Celia's name. I was angry. I had to leave the agency. I went for a walk and decided I was going to quit. I went back to the office and found her dead. The night we first met at the bar and I left, Jenna approached me needing a place to stay. You know the rest." Lucy could see that Duncan was exhausted. She suspected he had already been through a lifetime of hell in just a few short days.

"Duncan, tonight you can sleep in my bed. I will take the sofa. We will get some rest and go over all this again tomorrow. There are some things that are not sitting well with me and we may need to access the files on your computer. Do you think we can get back into the agency?" Lucy asked.

"Of course, I still have a key." Lucy walked over to the bedroom and opened the door. "Your room awaits." Lucy said.

"It smells like flowers." He took in a deep breath.

"It's my perfume. I think it's called Intrigue." She grabbed some clothes from the closet.

"That's fitting." Duncan reached over and caught the curl on her cheek. He slid it behind her ear.

"Goodnight Duncan, she pulled away.

"Goodnight Sweet Lucy,"

She went to the hall closet and pulled out a blanket, it would be the sofa for her tonight. She doubted however; she would get much sleep especially with everything that had transpired that evening. The other reason crept into her mind as she snuggled under her blanket. Duncan would sleep in her bed. That was enough to keep any girl wound up tight. Lucy did the only thing she could do, and that was look for another old movie on television to take her mind off things.

Chapter 13

The smell of bacon filled the room and honestly woke Lucy up from her restless night of sleep.

"Good morning." Duncan said happily as he placed the newly popped up toast on the plate. "I made breakfast for us." Lucy moaned and wanted to pull the cover up over her head.

"I am surprised that you found anything in there to eat. I bought that bacon for BLT's." She yawned as she peeked out.

"I was thinking last night about those files. I can access them quickly. I have Melinda's password and will be ready to give you whatever you need." He said confidently.

"Alright we will head up there after breakfast. Thank you for cooking." She tasted the salty bacon, and it seemed to melt in her mouth. When she finished the last savory bite, she went to put her plate in the sink. She accidentally brushed up against him.

Shifting nervously, he peered into her eyes.

"You are beautiful. Did you know that?" Duncan turned to the sink to rinse the dish. Lucy couldn't say anything, she was speechless. She felt compelled to touch him, she placed a hand on his back. She was scared. He seemed to bring out the boldness in her. He turned to look at her again.

She traced the buttons on his dress shirt with her fingers as he leaned in for a kiss. Their tongues danced against each other passionately. Lucy took a step back.

"Wow, I can barely breathe." She said almost gasping for air.

"I am sorry. I shouldn't have done that. It is just that ever since I laid eyes on you. I was hooked." Lucy grabbed Duncan by the collar.

"Kiss me again." She demanded hungrily for more. He tasted delicious. The salty bacon mingled with the sweet pleasure making her senses go wild. She wanted those soft lips all over her body. It had been forever since she had felt such pleasure and she longed for the hot business assistant to put that mouth to work on her.

Lucy shivered as Duncan continued to kiss her neck. He opened her blouse. He released a breast and began kneading it like a hungry kitten. Lucy moaned with pleasure as he lowered his head to feast on the soft flesh.

He paused a moment and remembered something. A look of reason came over him.

"I need my wallet. I think I have protection in there." He said with a wicked smile. "When I find it, I hope you will be ready for all the naughty things I am going to do to you. I am going to devour every inch of you."

Lucy giggled nervously and watched him walk away into the bedroom. She stood frozen in the kitchen. She was unclear if whether she should follow or stay.

"Lucy, where are you?" Duncan called from the bedroom with a seductive growl to his voice. She blushed and walked rather shyly to the door. He was shirtless and posing in nothing but his briefs.

"Come in here, I am ready for you. Let me watch you undress?" Lucy swallowed hard. The desire of his green eyes was burning into her skin. What was she doing? She had not been with a man in a long time. With every ounce of her courage gone, she wondered if she should run out of the room. Playing around was one thing, she could control that part.

She had trouble with this part. Kirk popped into her mind. She was lousy in bed and that is why he slept with Arlene. Here was a new "Oh shit" moment. She could not trust herself to say no to him. He had put a spell on her.

Duncan almost wondered where she was at, her eyes were glazed in a far off look. He was standing there and then confusion and fear crept into her face. She needed him to take control. He rose from the bed and walked over to her.

"Are you scared? You're not so tough now, are you?" She looked away as he moved, closing the distance between them. He took her mouth and claimed it once more with an erotic kiss. The humiliation burned her cheeks with embarrassment, but desire seemed to battle for its place as well.

"Close your eyes." He demanded softly. She could feel every erotic touch of his fingertips as they danced on her skin. Before too long her mind was dull and pleasure was taking over her body.

Lucy could feel her senses heightened as he slowly undressed her. Feathery soft kisses melted into her skin. Moaning softly was all she could do when he touched her lips with his.

"Come over to the bed." Duncan said softly still directing her every move. Something in him stirred. Never had any woman allowed him to take over this freely. Maybe he should back away. Give her a chance to get a hold of herself. He reasoned out in his head that he needed to stop but something inside of him urged him on.

Standing there exposed, caused her to shiver in his presence. She put her brain on auto-pilot and let him take control. Lucy slid into the bed next to him and felt a warm feeling pass over her. Duncan took his time exploring every inch of her body. Her nervousness soon faded away when they began making love. He was a careful lover and thought of everything. Right down to making sure they used protection.

Lucy relished in the sweetness of his touch. She had not felt this good in a long time. When they both finished he pulled her close and whispered into her ear.

"Thank you, sweet Lucy." Duncan nuzzled the back of her neck.

"I should be the one thanking you." She said.

Rolling over in bed, she faced him. She peered into his green eyes for a moment.

"Do you think that Melinda really could run a baby selling business?" She asked as the questions swirled in her mind.

"Really, I give you stellar love-making and you want to talk about my boss? You are indeed an interesting woman." He couldn't help but notice her lips were begging to be kissed again. He moved in and placed his lips on hers.

"Oh no you don't!" Lucy playfully pushed him back. "We have work to do. I have got to get to the office and check out those files. We have to figure this out or Jenna could be in danger." Lucy pulled the soft quilt around her and went to the bathroom to freshen up.

Duncan watched as she left the room.

"My Gosh that was amazing." He sighed adjusting himself back on the pillow. He could get used to waking up next to that sweet brown headed beauty with electric blue eyes. Excitement welled up over the fact the next few days they would be together.

He couldn't wait to find out more about her. When he emerged from the bathroom, he couldn't help but notice something he did not notice before. On her right shoulder was a scar. Suddenly he felt protective of her.

"What happened to your shoulder?" He asked his voice laced with concern. Lucy looked over her shoulder.

"My mother's boyfriend came at me with a knife. I think I was about eleven when it happened." She said it so matter-of-factly Duncan was surprised. He sat there and was wondering if he should pry further.

"Are you going to get dressed? Are you going to lay there and stare at me all day? I know I am beautiful but come on." She teased him lightly. He picked up one of her accent pillows and tossed it at her. He didn't pry about the scar. He would find out about her childhood later.

He took his turn in the bathroom and dressed quickly. Lucy handed him a cup of coffee and they left to do some digging at the office.

Chapter 14

Lucy stepped into the elevator with Duncan close behind her and pushed the number five on the light up panel. The office building was the largest in town and gave the city a medium thriving feel to it. Really though the town was smaller than it tried to be. The office building held several boutiques and businesses, but everyone knew that on the top floor was the Wishful Hearts Adoption Agency.

When the doors opened, Lucy heard a noise. No one should be up there. She pulled out her small .22 pistol. She pushed Duncan back behind her and stepped off the elevator. He followed behind wishing he had a Louisville Slugger to take out any potential danger. He didn't have a gun. Hell, he would probably shoot himself but a bat would work. He could protect Lucy. Although, she was carrying so she could protect them both.

He tried to be a little less old-fashioned but sometimes his male protector brain took over. She was quite a woman and could take care of herself. They cleared the rooms on the fifth floor. When they arrived in front of Melinda's office, they could tell someone had trashed it.

"I wonder what happened here." Lucy opened the door and walked in.

"It looks like someone was looking for something." Duncan walked over immediately to the file cabinet. He opened the drawers and several files were missing.

"What's wrong?" Lucy watched Duncan as he was staring at the drawers.

"There are some files missing. I know this because those files were the ones that were all on my list to check out. I haven't had the time, but I'm sure they're gone." Duncan shook his head. He left the office and went to his desk. Lucy watched in amazement while he sat down and began going through drawers.

"What are you doing?" She said curiously.

"I am downloading all the computer files that I had recently backed up on the new server. Every time someone would start the adoption process, I would scan the paperwork into the computer and save it. It is more efficient this way. Melinda never appreciated this part of my job. She said that it was a waste of time and she loved the paper trail." Duncan finished downloading the files on a flash drive and stuck them in his pocket. "Somebody killed Melinda and Early. I'm not stupid. I am the only surviving link to this case."

Lucy watched as he stuck another flash drive into the USB port.

"I am making several of these backups." He said.

Lucy watched him and wondered if he were being a little paranoid. She shrugged her shoulders and let him work.

In the quiet room, she heard the slight squeak of the elevator cable. She grabbed Duncan and pulled him into the storage closet.

"Someone's coming." Lucy placed her finger to her own lips signaling him to be quiet.

She could see through a small hole in the door. A woman got off the elevator, she looked a little disheveled and was very wary of her surroundings. She held a can of pepper spray in her hands. Most likely in case she ran into any intruders. When she was through poking around in Melinda's office, she left back on the elevator.

"Did she look familiar?" Lucy asked Duncan.

"No, I've never seen her. What do you think she wanted?" He wondered.

I think the same thing everyone in this town wants. Those files in your hands. If there are illegal adoptions taking place there are going to be many people wanting to hide it."

Lucy took one of the flash drives and placed it for safe keeping in her pocket. She watched as Duncan placed the other one in his. The other two were dropped in her bag.

"Let's go back to my office and check these out." Lucy said.

MILO LOOKED OVER AT his cell phone. Looking around and making sure that no one he knew was watching him, he took the call. A tiny grin crept upon his face.

"Kelsey, how are you? I will meet you there soon." Milo erased the number immediately from his phone just like he had done so many times before. Squaring things away with his assistant, he grabbed his briefcase and headed out the door. He looked up at the setting sun. Picking up his cell phone once again, he called Sydney.

"Hey babe, I am going to be a little late tonight. I have some work to do." Milo gave her the same excuse every single week for the last nine months. He hated to deceive Sydney, but he was falling in love with her best friend.

He had tried to end things several times. In fact, Kelsey threw a few monkey wrenches in their relationship too. They were just too drawn to each other. They always had been. Here lately, meeting up with Kelsey was the highlight of his week.

Sydney was pushing him further and further away. Ever since Jake took his life last year, Sydney shut herself away from the world and had become bitter. They were now even sleeping in separate beds. She was mean to him and everyone else.

Kelsey didn't waver though. No matter how hard and mean Sydney was to her, she still hung in there. She was just so beautiful. Kelsey listened to him and held him many nights when Sydney was in the hospital suffering from severe depression.

He pulled into the parking lot in his black town car. Right away he saw the small compact car that belonged to Kelsey. It was a good thing that this motel kept a room handy for him and was very discrete. He tapped on the door and waited for it to open. She pulled him inside and planted a long kiss.

"Milo, I have missed you." Kelsey whispered in his ear. He gave her bottom a little squeeze and sat his briefcase on the floor.

"I missed you too." He responded. "Did you see Sydney today?"

"I sure did, we had lunch together. This new therapist seems to be helping. I almost can see glimpses of my best friend again. I really miss my best friend, Milo. I think she is suspecting I am hiding something from her. I just don't want to hurt her." Kelsey swiped a tear falling from her cheek.

"I never meant to put you in this position. We can end this. I would never want to you to incur Sydney's wrath. Believe me, I have been there." Milo placed a comforting hand on her shoulder and pulled her close to his chest.

"I know. But you are just as important to me as Sydney is. I love you both, and that is so screwed up about this affair. I am just finding it harder and harder to look her in the eye and not be able to tell her how I feel." Kelsey said sadly.

"I know sweetheart. We didn't plan for this to happen."

"I sometimes wonder when and if she gets better. Are you going back to Sydney? Where do I stand Milo? Elections are coming up soon and I got to know."

"God Kelsey, do you honestly think this is easy for me? I love you. You know, but I made a promise to Sydney. I can't just walk away from her. Not now. What kind of man would I be?"

"The man that stood up for himself. The kind that was honorable."

"Isn't that kind of like the pot calling the kettle black? Really Kelsey, she would be just as hurt to find out that her best friend is meeting her husband once a week for a tryst."

"Well fine! If this is a tryst, I know now where I stand. Go to hell Milo!" Kelsey picked up her briefcase and left. Milo sunk down on the bed. This was turning out to be a horrible night. Now he had to go home to the ice queen.

Chapter 15

Sydney walked up the stairs and stood outside the door. The memories always flooded back and if she had any chance of fighting off the demons that plagued her. She would go into the room. Her therapist told her it would be good for her. It would help her heal. The sign on the door said 'keep out' and she had heeded its warning for the past year. She just could not bring herself to go in. It was a place her baby Jake, a dark brooding teenager, once inhabited.

He committed suicide, nothing could change the past. She placed her hand on the knob. It looked clean. Not like the day she walked in and found him dead amongst the dirty laundry and screaming, angry music blaring from his mp3 player. It became the worst day in her life.

Sydney took a step inside. Things were put away neatly. It was not a typical teenager's room. Milo must have cleaned it up. She remembered the blood covering the floor and the gun lying nearby. Everything else was hazy after that. They kept saying the word suicide and still to this day she was not sure it ever fully registered.

She went to the closet. Hanging up was Jake's favorite T-shirt. It had "The Crushers" printed on it. She grabbed the shirt and sobbed as she sunk down on his bed. So many emotions just flooded out of her. It surprised her at how much she felt. Sydney decided not to hold the emotions back anymore.

She was tired of being miserable. She was tired of her marriage being on the edge of destruction. Milo was now sleeping in the guest room. Her bed was just so lonely at night. To make things worse, she also suspected that he was having an affair. She knew who was keeping her husband's time too. Kelsey had become a fixture in Milo's life. Things had become so complicated. Every Wednesday, like clockwork, he worked late.

Just like every Wednesday evening, Kelsey would become unavailable, with her cell phone shut off. She wondered if she should let them know she was not stupid. However; Sydney often blamed herself. She knew they were in the wrong but she ended up pushing two very lonely people into each other's arms. Kelsey was Jake's Godmother, and the news of his suicide destroyed her as well.

She missed them both in her life. After her therapy session today, she needed to put the pieces of her life back into their rightful places. Sydney was going to fight for her husband and get her best friend back. She was going to give them the chance to do the right thing. Then if they didn't, she would just have to force the issue.

She needed to release some baggage in her life. She stood up from the bed and placed the shirt back into the closet. Closing the door behind her, she felt a little better.

"I'm home." Milo called from downstairs. Sydney rushed to greet him.

"I am so glad you are here. I missed you." She threw her arms around him.

"Are you alright?" Milo asked carefully.

"I am fine. Let's order a pizza and watch a movie. You know, like we used to do while we were dating." Milo looked at his wife and saw the sparkle return to his eyes.

"Sure Syd, let me get changed. I want to hear about your day. It sounds like you had a great one."

"For the first time in a year, I feel like my old self." Sydney pulled out a movie and went and popped popcorn.

DUNCAN TYPED IN THE password and all the files opened. Lucy stood beside him in amazement.

"You're telling me that these files here are separate from the files you have?" She asked.

"Yes, Melinda did a good job making sure she hid things. I can go through and help you decipher these if you like. I am curious what is in these files myself. Some of them look a little questionable."

"You're a genius Duncan." Lucy pulled up a chair beside him.

"First, we have to agree on something." he said.

"What's?" She looked at him curiously.

"I will get access for you to look at these files, but I need to know that you are not going to use these files to harm people. What's done is done." Duncan's eyes were serious, and she hadn't thought about how much power she had at her fingertips.

These were people's lives. Good people at that. She was no expert. She didn't have a clue on how to tell which adoptions were fabricated and which ones were legitimate.

"I just want to clear Jenna, Early and you from this mess. So only open the ones that you think are questionable. The rest we will turn over to the FBI for them to investigate."

"Fair enough." Duncan began working on some list and categorizing some ones pertaining to the case.

"Early said something about the mayor's wife. Can you pull the files for Milo and Sydney out?"

Duncan opened the case file and read.

"They gave Melinda two-hundred thousand dollars to find them a male baby. Jake's mother was a drug addict, but that info wasn't disclosed in the public records. According to the notes here, Sydney tried several times to have the file unsealed for medical purposes. Melinda must have refused because the documents were ignored." Lucy looked on in fascination.

"It could've been that Sydney found out and retaliated. She could've come after Melinda."

"It could be. But how would she have known? These documents are sealed. Someone would have had to tell her." Duncan reasoned.

"Who was Jake's birth parents? Maybe they surfaced."

"It says here his mother was a drug addict and in prison. His father is unknown."

"I think we need to start here. Let's go talk to the birth mother." Duncan shook his head in agreement. He looked over at her scribbling notes in her notebook.

"You know I can set up your computer to help you with your business." He smiled at her, trying to take notes quickly.

"I'm good with paper. It never lets me down." Duncan stood up and stretched. He walked over to where she was sitting.

"Can we talk about us now?" he asked. Lucy put her pencil down and stared into his green eyes.

"I need to tell you I loved this morning but, I am not sure. I mean, we barely know one another." Duncan said.

"I know. It just happened. I am glad it is out of our system and we can get down to work." Lucy turned away. She didn't want him to see the hurt in her eyes. Fear crept from somewhere dark inside her. Things were awkward between them. A one-night stand was all they had.

"Lucy, you don't understand. I want to know you better. I am not the man that sleeps with a woman and then can walk away. I have feelings for you. I am not sure what kind yet, but I know I want to be with you." Lucy nervously shifted in her seat. Was he talking about a romance with her? There was no way that she would even define what they had.

"Duncan, let's just be who we are. We don't need to get wrapped up and call it anything other than friendship yet." She said with a sigh.

"Alright, if that is what you want. We will be friends. Goodnight." She watched him leave the room with a dejected scowl.

Lucy leaned back in her office chair. Feelings were brewing inside of her too, but she would not allow them to manifest. At least not until all the craziness was over.

Chapter 16

Milo Harper woke up to his cell phone buzzing frantically on his night-stand. He looked over at his beautiful wife sleeping. She had finally let him back into bed with her. Last night was amazing, and it had been forever since they stayed up talking and making love until dawn. Quickly though, the other dilemma popped into his head. He looked at his phone and saw a message from Kelsey. It merely said, I am sorry.

Sydney moaned and opened her eyes.

"Good Morning, sweetheart. I hoped that you would still be here." Sydney said.

"I wanted to wake up next to my beautiful wife. Thank you for last night." He wrapped his arms around her.

"Milo, are you having an affair? I mean, I know I am horrible to live with lately. I have been spiraling out of control since Jake. I should have never driven you away. I am sorry." She said with promise in her misty eyes.

"No, I love you and only you. Wednesday nights are only work related. I swear! I will make more of an effort to be home with you." Milo closed his eyes and prayed that would be all she asked. He was just contented when Sydney placed her head on his chest.

Bingo, she thought. Now he would have to blow Kelsey off. She kissed his bare chest and smiled. Later today, she would confront Kelsey.

LUCY WOKE UP. THERE was no coffee or bacon cooking. She wondered if Duncan was still asleep. Walking to the door of her bedroom, she tapped light-ly. She needed some clothes from the closet. She opened the door and peeked in. He was not there. Looking at her clock, she wondered where he had gone. Maybe perhaps he was out for a walk or something. Something bad could have happened to him. He knew a lot about the agency.

"Crap!" Didn't he have sense enough to know that he was in danger?

Grabbing her cell phone, she dialed his number. As it rang, he came through the door. She snapped her phone off and rolled her eyes.

"Good Morning," he said cheerfully.

"Where have you been? I was worrying." She said in annoyance.

"I went to the store and bought food. You have none. Do you know you eat like crap?" He said while putting away some vegetables in the refrigerator.

"I like the way I eat. Besides, I am not sure why you care. Do you know you are a target? You should have taken me with you." She said.

"Sweet Lucy, contrary to what you think, I care. Also, I am a big boy and I can take care of myself." He said with a smirk on his lips.

"Fine. Do whatever you wish." She shrugged her shoulders and crossed her arms in defiance. She eyed him curiously as he crept toward her. Holding her ground, she noticed he had that look. You know the one where she would end up back in her bed moaning his name in pleasure again.

"You make me crazy." Duncan moved closer to her. "Why do I terrify you? You are shivering." He placed a hand on her shoulder.

"I don't know." She answered quickly and turned away. Duncan pulled her close and tilted her chin up. He planted a long, warm kiss upon her lips. Lucy pulled away.

"I have to get a shower before I go." Running into the bathroom, she locked the door behind her. Leaning up against it, she sighed. Nothing with Duncan made any sense. How could she be falling for a man she barely even knew? He would creep into her mind at the most inopportune times. Ever since he touched her, that was all she could think about.

"Get a grip, Lucy." She muttered to herself as she stepped into a cool shower.

MILO WALKED INTO THE coffee shop and ordered his usual black coffee. Kelsey was sitting in the familiar spot where they met every morning. He walked over to her and sat across from her.

"I wasn't sure you would be here. If I knew we were meeting, I would've ordered you a coffee." She said lightly.

"Me neither. I don't want to hurt you, but we need to end this. I can't keep two women happy in my life. I will end up destroying you both. You deserve better, Kelsey. I'm sorry."

"Milo, I am not sure I want to end this. Can we be more discreet? I love you." She swallowed hard, fighting off tears. Milo could see her heart breaking right in front of him. He felt like a worthless dog now. He was sitting across from a woman who he had no business being with in the first place.

"Sydney has had a break through and she is feeling better. She suspects me having an affair. If she catches on, you will lose your friendship. I can't be the one to be in the middle of something so beautiful. Sydney told me last night she cherished your friendship." Milo sipped his coffee. She sat staring down at the table. He touched her cheek.

"Kelsey, I am sorry I did this to you. We knew there was going to come a day when this would end. Did you honestly think I could ever be with you?" He asked quietly.

"Yes, I was under the delusion that you might actually love me too. You said you did. I guess the skilled politician lied. I should've known." She hurled the insult at him.

"I do, but things are complicated. You can't expect me to walk away from Sydney and my career." He tried to reason with her.

"Yes, Milo, things are complicated. You are right. You no longer have to worry about me complicating your life any further." She stood up and grabbed her purse.

"Have a nice fucking life!" She yelled at him as she left the coffee shop.

LUCY STEPPED OUT INTO the bright sunlight. It felt good against her skin. She got into her car and turned over the engine. She looked up when the door opened.

"Duncan, what are you doing?" She asked.

"I am going with you to the prison. We are a team and I want to help you with this." He settled himself on the seat next to her. She watched him trying to shut the door.

"Pull the handle up and slam it." She said.

"Nice car. I don't think I have ever seen one that came from the circus." Duncan chuckled.

"When you're done making fun of my car, you can exit. I don't think that this is such a good idea for you to go. You are too exposed out in the open." She waited for him to exit her vehicle.

"I am going. You will not get rid of me that easily. Besides, I always wanted to ride around in a clown car." He said with a seductive grin as he brushed against her arm. She only wished that she could squish the tingles into a safe little box somewhere and hide them.

They mostly rode in silence. When they saw the high barbed wire fence, they knew they were getting close to the prison. There were guards armed everywhere. Duncan looked a little nervous. Finally, she might could gain the upper hand.

"Pretty scary place, huh." Duncan said. For him to be so bold with his advances with her, he looked as though that he wanted to scurry off like a little mouse and hide. Somehow even his own discomfort was charming in a way. Duncan stayed close by as they walked to the front of the prison.

"Stay close. Follow instructions. Say nothing. This is a different world. I would hate for you to get gutted on your first day out solving a mystery." She watched him as he was shaking his head nervously. He was indeed speechless. She chuckled softly. She wasn't sure she was ready to admit that she was only kidding.

She couldn't help but turn away and smile. The guards buzzed her into a visiting room. They waited for several minutes. The door buzzed again and Jessie De Tores entered the room. Her eyes were hard and her black braid hung over her shoulder. Tattoos covered her skin, barely leaving room for the flesh color to come through. Lucy could tell life wasn't easy on the woman.

"Jessie, my name is Lucy. I was wondering if we could talk to you about a case." Lucy could feel Duncan shift nervously beside her.

"Are you a cop? I don't talk to cops." She muttered.

"No, I work in private investigations to be exact. I wanted to ask you a few questions if you aren't too busy." Lucy handed her a business card.

"What's with scared-y cat over here? He looks like I'm fixing to hit him." Jessie laughed.

"He always looks like that. Takes life way too seriously." Lucy nudged him in the ribs playfully. He needed to lighten up.

"Ask me anything. I ain't got nowhere to go." Jessie said, leaning back in her chair.

"I hate to bring up painful memories, but I have recently run across some paperwork that you had placed a baby up for adoptions with the Wishful Hearts Adoption Agency. Do you remember anything about that experience?" Lucy asked.

"I am not so sure I want to talk about it." Jessie said quietly. Moisture dotted the corners of her sad eyes.

"Look Jessie, I know this is painful. Honestly, this place scares the hell out of me. My name is Duncan and I am just trying to stay alive. Lucy is protecting me now. I just need to know if you remember Melinda Hartgrove. Did she do anything questionable?" Duncan said in a compassionate voice.

"I hate that woman. She stole my baby. I was eighteen when I had him and was living on the streets. Melinda threatened to kill me. When I reported her to the police, they arrested me on the spot and took my baby away. They sentenced me with twenty years in a drug charge." She retorted. "It was my first offense."

"That seems to be a little excessive." Lucy said.

"Did she force you to sign any documents?" Duncan interrupted.

"No, I couldn't read or write until I came to prison. I am going to make something of myself when I get out in five more years." She said proudly.

"That is great. I wish you the best. Let me give you my card. I would love to check in on you from time to time if that's alright." Lucy touched her hand warmly.

"Sure, that would be real nice. I don't have many friends." Jessie took the card and placed it in her pocket.

"Consider me a new friend. Did anyone else come to see you about the baby since you have been here?" Lucy asked.

"Some woman told me her son was in trouble. Said she was a mayor's wife of some town called Sentry. Anyway, she told me her son had just died. Wanted to meet me because I was the kid's biological mother. She was sad. I looked at the picture. Jake had my eyes. But that precious boy had some problems and killed himself. She was asking if there was a history of mental illness in my family." Jessie bit her bottom lip. "I told her mama killed herself when I was a teenager. She left crying." The woman sighed deeply.

"Thanks Jessie, you have helped so much. Will you look at a picture for me? Is this the woman who came to visit you?" Lucy placed the picture in front of her.

"Nah, that ain't her? This woman had brown hair. Her eyes were further apart, and the lips were all wrong." She said as she stood up and left the room. Lucy thanked her and they left the prison building.

Chapter 17

"Boy, you got over your fear. It was nice of you to donate some money to her fund." Lucy said as she headed the car back to town.

"Another one of Melinda's victims, I hate she took advantage of innocent girls. It makes me angry. I only took the job to help people, and she tainted the entire process." Duncan looked out the window with disappointment. Lucy could see he was upset. It made her feel sad.

"What made you want to take a job at an adoption agency?" Lucy asked curiously.

"My sister. She found out early in her marriage that she was infertile. Her and her husband tried hard to have a baby. All the hope and dreams dashed with each treatment that they went through and failed. Well anyway, they adopted. Bridget has been in ours for six years and she is the cutest child." Duncan pulled out a picture and Lucy looked at it while driving.

"She is a little doll. I bet she loves her Uncle Duncan." Lucy said.

"That's why this whole Melinda situation is so disturbing. Melinda ripped those babies from their mothers and justified it by saying they would be better off. It just sickens me. The women didn't even have a choice." He said with disgust.

"I agree. Of course, there are women out there that would've given up their kids. My mother did." Lucy said offhandedly.

"I am sorry, Lucy. I know your childhood must have been horrific." Duncan remembered the scar on her shoulder.

"My mother was one of those women who didn't want children. I was a mistake. A huge one. My aunt Bertie raised me. Most of my memories about my mother are not great." Lucy said soberly.

"Your aunt sounds like a wonderful person." Duncan said.

"She was wonderful. She straightened me out, gave me a chance to become my own person. I never would have had a chance if she didn't raise me." Lucy said.

"That's wonderful. You are an amazing woman. You were so kind to Jessie as well." Duncan said.

"Duncan, tell you what, after the crappy day we have had let's stop here for some ice-cream." Lucy smiled, hoping it would cheer the both of them up. She pulled into the parking lot. The teenage girl behind the counter, wearing a chocolate smudged apron and pin hat, took their order. They waited for the ice cream and took their seats across the room with little latticed white metal chairs.

"I never would have taken you for the Rocky Road type of girl". I figured you were more of a mint chocolate chip." He teased lightly.

"Oh, I have to hear this. I did not know there were 'ice cream' types of people." She said.

"Of course, ice cream preference is like looking into the soul of someone. Like that lady over there." He pointed to a woman spooning chocolate-covered cherry ice cream. "She is a mom, I bet. You can tell. She closes her eyes with each bite and savors it slowly. That means she is escaping. No cone, likes a bowl. She doesn't like the mess. Probably has small children at home. When she has had enough, she gets a sitter. She gets her hair done and comes here before returning to her life." She looked over at him, engaged in his thoughts.

"Wow she says, you are right. How wild? Are you psychic?" The red headed woman asked.

"No, just know my ice cream." Duncan said.

"I am next, do me." A big burly man said. Duncan looked close at his cone. "Cookie dough, you are a man of your own. Probably own several bikes. Likes to feel the wind in your hair. Also you miss your mom, she probably baked chocolate chip cookies a lot for you. You come here to pay memory to her by eating cookie dough ice cream." Duncan said.

"Actually close man, my Grams. She sent me cookies once a week." The biker man clad in leather said.

"Wow, you are full of surprises. I have never heard of anyone with this gift before. But wasn't those kind of simple choices." Lucy teased.

Duncan's eyes went dark. "You know what I can tell about you Sweet Lucy? Rocky Road is tough. It is dark but with lots of yummy secrets hidden beneath its creamy layer. It makes love as hard as it chases bad guys. It causes men to not know what has hit them once they're entangled with you." Lucy swallowed hard and felt warmness engulf her.

She needed to switch to a nice vanilla ice cream. Rocky Road was going to get her in trouble. Duncan smiled noticing her squirm.

"You don't say." That was all that she could squeak out. She changed subjects after a few awkward moments of silence. They walked to the car and got in. She needed to go back to the office and try to do some research. So many questions were still unanswered around in her brain.

"If Sydney was not the one who saw Jessie, who could have visited her?" She wondered out loud.

"You know how women change their hair color. It could have been her but Jessie didn't recognize her." Duncan finished up the last bit of his vanilla and chocolate swirled ice-cream.

"No I don't think so. She seemed adamant. Maybe it was somebody standing in for her. She is pretty recognizable." Lucy said. "Sydney is one of those women who has a certain look. She is pretty porcelain. She is really quite beautiful."

Lucy's phone rang the theme song from a movie called Creature's From Within.

Duncan's eyebrow raised in fascination. The little short answers she spoke into the phone captivated him. She quickly ended her call with annoyance plastered on her face.

"I have a meeting later. It's kind of private so I will drop you off at my place you can hang out there until I get back. Please stay there, I don't want to worry about you." She said.

"Is everything alright?" Duncan said with concern.

"Yep fine. I just have to handle up on something from my past. You know one of those 'secret rocky road' things." She smiled at him and dropped him off at the door.

What in the world could Kirk possibly want? It was a bad break up and she was angry for such a long time. They tried to remain partners for a while and then Lucy just eventually quit. She couldn't stand working on the Police force with him. He got a promotion. She hated the fact that he was now in a power of position.

Lucy walked into the bar. Cooper's was always buzzing this time of night. The pool tables were busy with the local college kids blowing off steam. The other room to the right had large screen televisions tuned in for many sporting events.

"Hello Paul." Lucy said jovially.

"Hey, princess. How was your date the other night? Did you have fun?" Paul wiped the bar with a towel.

"It was alright. Have you seen Kirk around?" Lucy asked.

"Yeah in the back. You know where." He waved his hands toward the television room.

Paul handed her two bottles, and she went to find Kirk. When she found him sitting in the room's corner watching the game intently, memories flooded back. Things were not always so bad between them. They used to sit cuddled on the oversized leather chair watching football together. She swallowed hard and try to push the memory from her mind. She lowered the bottle from behind him in front of his face.

"Thanks babe." he said not turning around.

"Who you calling Babe?" Lucy teased.

"I thought you were Jenny. Glad you're here. I need to talk to you." Lucy sucked in a breath when he placed his hand on the small of her back. She hated the way he touched her. Sometimes it was still way too intimate. They walked to a secluded table toward the back of the bar.

"What's up Kirk? Why all the privacy?" She tried to be direct.

"Milo called, he's got a problem. I need an answer from a woman's perspective." Kirk said.

"Why don't you ask Arlene? She is much more of a woman than I am, remember."

"Please don't start. That was awhile ago and I've moved on." Kirk said.

"You're right. I don't want to fight. Besides, I have moved on too." Lucy bit her bottom lip.

"Congrats, who is the lucky devil?" He said with jealousy.

"Duncan." She was not sure why she said it. Perhaps she was tired of Kirk pitying her after he ruined her for other men.

"You mean the nerdy guy from the adoption agency. He's not your type. It'll never last." He said taking a drink from his beer. Lucy rolled her eyes.

"What, are you jealous? I mean you left me. How do you know what my type is?" Lucy said.

"Maybe I am a little. But you need to remember you're the one who didn't want to marry me. A geek is not your type, sweetheart." Kirk said angrily as he grabbed her arm.

She had seen that look of fire on his face before and she tried to keep the old feelings from rising to the top. "I loved you. Lord help me, I still do sometimes." He released her arm.

Lucy looked down at her hands. He was right. When he asked, she turned him down. Life was crazy then. Aunt Bertina was dying in the nursing home and she didn't want the same thing to happen to her, that happened to her mother. Her mother had lost herself and Lucy determined to be her own woman and not let any man control her. She didn't want Kirk to control her. She needed time. However; Kirk's time was not hers. He wouldn't wait. She quickly found out why when he found him with Arlene.

"What's Milo's problem?" She asked with an exasperated sigh. Desperately wanting to change the subject and get this whole meeting over with. A year seemed like a lifetime in some areas and nothing in others.

"Well Sydney has had a hard time since Jake's suicide. She apparently has been looney lately if you know what I mean." He rolled his finger in circles around his head. "Anyway, apparently Milo got involved with another woman. Sydney's best friend to be exact. Anyway, since Sydney's better now they have worked things out and Milo's ended things with Kelsey."

"Okay, what's the problem?" Lucy said.

"Well Milo needs someone to go talk to Kelsey and make sure she is alright and make sure she will not smear his next campaign. This is where you come in. I trust you to be discrete and maybe you could help with this little fiasco before it gets out of hand and we lose the mayor. You can relate you were in her shoes."

"Seriously!" Lucy rolled her eyes in disgust. "Number one, we are not in eighth grade anymore. Geez! I don't even know this Kelsey woman. What makes you think she is going to open and share? Number two maybe this needs to be a lesson to men around the world to not be cheaters. You have really taken the cake on this one. How stupid is this entire conversation?"

"I screwed up. I just thought you could have a man bashing evening, eat ice cream and she could get over Milo. I'm trying to just help my buddy out." Kirk tipped his beer bottle back for another swig.

"The answer is no! Besides, you're so worried about it, why don't you go talk to her yourself. Oh wait. Milo is trying to do the right thing. Why in the hell would you possibly think that I would talk to Milo's lover about moving on? Maybe you need to make Arlene talk to her." Lucy stood up and headed for the door angrily.

Chapter 19

He really had some nerve. She thought to herself. She opened the door to her apartment. Jinx skittered out like his usual self. Throwing her keys on the entry way table, the aroma from the kitchen caused her stomach to protest in hunger. She tried to put on a pleasant demeanor for Duncan.

"It smells great." Lucy said as she watched him stirring pots.

"I used to be a cook in a diner before I went to school for Administrative Assisting. I love to cook." Lucy watched on and made small talk.

The phone rang and interrupted them their conversation. Lucy answered it.

"I know you know where Jenna and the baby are. If you don't tell me, I will kill your boyfriend."

The voice paused. "Who is this?" Lucy demanded.

"Make your choice. With all the secrets in this town, maybe we should share a bunch of yours. Your mother was a whore. How would Duncan like to know about that? You will have until midnight tomorrow night to deliver me the baby and the mother at Colter's Park. If not, you and Duncan are dead. Look out your window. I mean business. I will call with further instructions."

The voice was chilling, and the line went dead. Carefully she walked over to the window and peeked around the curtain. A bomb sent vibrations under the house as the night sky lit up before her. Car alarms sounded off all around the area.

"No, My car!" She ran down the stairs of her building screaming. Duncan followed close behind her.

"Go back!" she screamed. "Call the police." Sirens sounded off in the vicinity in minutes that seemed like an eternity.

Chief Kirk was on the scene first. He jumped out of the truck and hurried to her.

"What the hell happened? Are you alright?" He asked with grave concern on his face.

"I'm not sure. I got a phone call that asked me about Jenna and Andrew. She also threatened to kill Duncan." Duncan moved protectively closer to Lucy.

Lucy leaned into Duncan allowing his arms to engulf her with his protective hold.

"It's alright." He said lovingly. "Just stay here, sweet Lucy." He whispered comforting her.

Kirk kept staring at the man embracing his ex-girlfriend. A twinge of jealousy rose from his stomach.

"Don't I know you? You look familiar man." Kirk looked him over good.

"Damn, it is you. The famous Duncanator." The two men high-fived each other.

"Kirkster, is this where you landed, man? Sweet! Police Chief. I didn't know you were here." Lucy watched on in utter confusion and was curious how they knew one another. They sounded like they were the best of friends and obviously had some strange sort of male language.

"You are the Duncan that Lucy is protecting. I thought you were a nerdy computer guy. She was telling me earlier about you. I can see now she was delusional." Kirk laughed.

Duncan shrugged his shoulders with a grin on his face.

"What is that supposed to mean, delusional?" Lucy said indignantly, as she placed her hands defiantly on her hips.

"Honey, you mean you don't know. This guy is a legend. We were in college together. He's fearless. He was wrestling champ in our school. Took out five guys in a barroom brawl one time, he's got some skills that would make you beg for mercy. The women, well let's just say a lot of hearts were broken back home." Lucy rolled her eyes. It figures, one more reason to stay away from him.

A few days ago, she didn't even know Duncan and still, yet he was just as confusing to her as Superman was to Lois Lane. He was a mild-mannered unemployed assistant by day with powers of seduction by night. A secret strong man in her midst that made her knees tremble and her body quake with desire.

He could read a person off their choice of ice cream. Had her world gone officially topsy-turvy?

"Kirk, I am making dinner upstairs. You want to join us? We can catch up on old times, man." Duncan asked. Lucy quickly remembered the little white lie she told to Kirk. She hated lying some people were good at it. She always felt like she was on the verge of throwing up.

"No, I don't think that is a good idea. Kirk is investigating whoever did this to my car." Lucy tried to reason. "He'll be busy. Right Kirk." She flashed him a warning look that Kirk ignored.

"No, I got time to hang out with the Duncanator. Besides the boys will do the cleanup. Let me call my girl and tell her I am having dinner here." Kirk sounded like a child calling to ask for permission from Arlene.

"Arlene, I promise there is someone here besides Lucy. The Duncanator is here. I know honey. Here talk to Lucy." Kirk pushed the phone into Lucy's hand. She looked at Kirk as if he were crazy.

"Tell her you and Duncan are an item, so she won't get jealous. Tell her what you told me tonight. She won't be threatened." Kirk said excitedly.

At this exact moment she could kill Kirk. Duncan was intrigued with the complexities of their relationships.

"Yes, Lucy. Tell Arlene what you told Kirk earlier. I would like to hear it myself." Duncan had a smirk of approval, she honestly got caught red-handed. She just hoped she would not lose her clothes on the bedroom floor later. She picked up the phone.

"Arlene, you know Kirk and I can barely stand each other. I will be really shocked if I make it through the night without killing him." She narrowed a glare his way. "I just had this great idea. You should come over and double with us. It will be fun." Lucy hung up and smiled at Kirk. She had a smile on her face when he looked as though someone had kicked him in a very private place.

"Arlene's on her way." She said to Kirk and received a nasty look.

"Why did you invite her? She will spend the night griping at me." Kirk said.

"Why should she miss out on all this fun?" Lucy smiled wickedly, "She is your girlfriend after all." Lucy gave an almost maniacal laugh and went up the stairs.

"Man, this ought to be an interesting night." Duncan said.

Chapter 20

Arlene breezed through the door dressed in a pink skirt, pink floral top and pink shoes. She looked like a bottle of tummy medicine. Frankly, just the thought of her made Lucy feel nauseated.

"I knocked, and no one heard me. So, I hope you don't mind me coming in." Arlene said sweetly with every ounce of charm she could muster.

"No honey. Come meet the Duncanator." Kirk introduced his wife to Duncan, and everyone made small talk. Lucy excused herself and went to the kitchen to grab a knife. She started stabbing a tomato violently cursing under her breath.

"How are you holding up? I, as your boyfriend deserve to know." A grin crept across Duncan's face.

"I am fine. I will explain later. Please don't rat me out. I have to save face." She spoke.

"Very interesting. We will talk soon." He said as he brushed his lips to hers and it sent chills to her toes. Lucy wished he would stop making her feel so vulnerable. Here she was caught in a sort of crazy triangle and she only hoped that she would wake up and it was all a dream. She felt like the famous Alice falling down a rabbit hole.

"You are just loving this aren't you?" Lucy seethed with color rising to her cheeks, embarrassed.

"Sweet Lucy. You're mine, at least for tonight. I am the happiest man on earth." He said with a charming grin.

"You know I am holding a knife, right?" Duncan laughed and pulled her into the living room to entertain her motley band of guests.

Some women would have retreated to their rooms and locked the door. She however, needed to stay and find out what happened. She should have the sense enough to jump out the window and hide. But Duncan's hand on hers felt like a rock. Maybe he sensed her panic. She peered at him talking out of the corner of her eyes.

The truth would soon come out and then Duncan would probably back off from her. She was sure that Kirk and Arlene would spill the story of her sordid past with them. That might be the only thing keeping her from bolting.

"Lucy is so amazing and helpful Arlene. I know someone with her caliber of training can keep me safe." Lucy watched him as he took Arlene by the hand. "You look like a woman that understands romance so you will know what I am saying. The moment I laid eyes on her I knew she was the one." Duncan leaned over and placed a tender kiss on Lucy's cheek.

Lucy rolled her eyes wondering if he was used to laying things on so thick with all the women in his life. Kirk mentioned Duncan was a player. Jealousy seeped up slowly from her stomach. Lucy could see that Arlene was eating up every word Duncan spoke.

"That is so sweet Duncan. I didn't ever think that Lucy would find anyone else. Kirk and she were almost engaged. I hate to say it, but I was the other woman. I am glad Lucy found happiness at last." Lucy wondered if she stood up and planted a kiss on Kirk, how fast Arlene's head would spin and pop off. Of course, watching Kirk shifting nervously in his chair made her giddy with utter delight. He didn't want to be in the spotlight any more than she did.

"Kirk, all I have to say is thanks man! Lucy could be nothing but the only one for me." Duncan placed another kiss on her soft lips this time deepening it more intimately. He asked Lucy for help in the kitchen.

"I know you are uncomfortable. I am sorry, I didn't know you and Kirk were all that serious." He plated the food.

"Laying it on a little thick, aren't we? I mean I do not think anyone has ever flattered me quite in that light." Lucy diverted her gaze shyly.

"You know you are worth it, right?" Duncan placed a finger under her chin and lifted it gently. "Kirk is in there squirming because he knows he lost the best thing that has ever happened to him." Lucy cleared her throat.

"Ancient history. I haven't been sitting here pining away for him if that is what you are thinking. It was a ten-year relationship that ended with him sleeping with Arlene because I turned him down on a marriage proposal. Most of what I feel is anger and revenge." Lucy said with a scowl as she carried the plates out of the kitchen.

"Look at this amazing food. It looks delicious." Arlene said as she took a baby carrot from her plate and sucked it into her mouth. Now she knew why Arlene was so popular with Kirk. Lucy seethed at Kirk. The meal was delicious. There was succulent roasted duck with plum sauce, fresh green beans seasoned to perfection and glazed baby carrots that melted in Lucy's mouth.

Several times she was so busy eating that she did not follow the conversation at the table. Her mind snapped back to attention when Kirk mentioned Early and Melinda.

"I guess you have to open the case back up now that someone bombed my car." Kirk looked across the table incredulously at her.

"I don't think the two are related. Early killed Melinda. I think there is someone gunning for Duncan because of the files at the office. Someone broke in and stole some of them. I just don't know which ones they took. Maybe Duncan can look and see." Kirk said.

"Poor Melinda." Arlene broke in sadly. "This town is in a fix. She was quite a wonderful and kind heart." Arlene said sadly.

"Melinda held some pretty powerful secrets. We have been uncovering them left and right. She was definitely no saint." Duncan said with anger rising in his voice.

"Well, if you have something to tell me. I will be happy to hear you out. I know Lucy would know better than to withhold evidence from the police." Kirk said as he chewed on a carrot.

"We have nothing." Lucy said quickly. "It's all here-say. Honey don't mistake rumor for facts. We're still investigating." She squeezed Duncan's leg tightly hopefully to silence him. She was glad when he got the message and changed the subject.

After they cleared the dinner dishes, he took his seat next to Lucy. There was an awkward silence in the room.

"Wow, it is getting late." Duncan yawned and looked at his watch with a subtlety in his voice. "Besides, I need a little alone time with my woman." Duncan said as he grabbed Lucy's hand playfully. Arlene giggled.

"Yes, Kirk let's get out of here and let Duncan and Lucy have some time together. Besides, I need some ice-cream Kirk. Thanks for the lovely meal." Arlene turned to Lucy. "You deserve happiness with all the crap we put you through. I'm sorry." Lucy almost fell over. Arlene was sincere.

"Arlene, no hard feelings. It was a different time." Lucy couldn't breathe when Arlene pulled her close in a hug. Kirk pulled Arlene away and said his final thanks and goodnight.

"Whew! I am glad that nightmare is over." Lucy said with her back against the closed door. She looked over at Duncan and sighed realizing that she owed him an explanation.

"Thank you, I shouldn't have told Kirk that we were together. I am glad you didn't blow my cover." Lucy said.

"It's alright. I'm sorry, I asked him to stay for dinner. I didn't know the situation." Duncan reached into the refrigerator and pulled out a cake. Lucy was in awe.

"It doesn't have to be a cover you know. I would still like to explore the options." Duncan cut a piece of Black Forest cake and slid it on her plate. She took a bite and was in heaven.

"My goodness, this is amazing. How did you know I would love this so much?" She was nearly in a pure state of chocolate bliss. He moved closer to her.

"Rocky Road, sweet Lucy." His eyes were daring her to respond.

"Wrestling huh, here I have been running around trying to figure out how to protect you." She said taking another bite.

"Well, I would be happy to show you some of my moves sweetheart. I think you and I entangled over there on that red rug might be kind of fun." He teased.

"I am sure you do," she said nervously.

"You're turning me on, just watching you enjoy that cake." He laughed lightly.

"Yes, it's true I have a love affair with chocolate." She responded.

He took his finger and dipped it into the icing. Walking over to where she was sitting, he tasted the icing and kissed her deeply. The room spun. His masterful hands slid from her neck to the top button of her blouse. He slowly released the top one. She was going to protest, and he covered her mouth with his, daring her to say anything. Trailing kisses to the top of her bra, she tried to make her brain say stop. Pushing him away, she gasped for air.

"We have to stop." She said breathlessly.

"Why?" He asked.

"Because I don't trust myself with you." Lucy stood up and buttoned her blouse.

"You will give in. Just so you know sweet Lucy, this is far from over. I never give up on what I want." Duncan kissed her lightly on the lips and took his leave to the bedroom.

Chapter 22

Lucy needed space. Duncan was going to break her heart like Kirk did. She left the apartment and went to her office. Opening her laptop, she saw what color hair the Mayor's wife had. There would be media pictures of her all over the place.

Sydney was a blonde and Lucy never remembered her ever being a brunette or a red head. Pictures of her and Milo popped up in the search. They also had various family pictures posted. She had to find a woman that was always around the mayor. A family member or friend. Then she could take them back to the prison and let Jessie have a look.

She printed off a family reunion picture. There was one picture that caught her eye. It was one of Milo, Sydney, and another woman on the beach with a young Jake. Lucy's mind remembered that Kirk mentioned that Sydney's best friend was Kelsey. Typing in the new name in the search engine, she found a picture of Kelsey, she was in the water splashing around with Jake.

"This must be who Milo is sleeping with behind Sydney's back. She couldn't help herself. She booed and hissed at the computer screen with a whisper.

Men are such asses, she thought to herself. She looked up and noticed Duncan watching her with amusement plastered on his face.

"What are you looking at?" He asked. Lucy explained her meeting with Kirk earlier in the day.

"The mayor surely has his hands full. I wonder how he keeps everything straight." Lucy looked at him puzzled.

"Relationships, two of them, would get complicated. Two birthdays. Two anniversaries. Wouldn't it all get confusing?" Duncan wondered.

"I don't know some men never have a problem." Lucy said flatly.

"Could you ever forgive Kirk? Why didn't you marry him?" Duncan asked curiously.

"I was scared too. I didn't want to end up some man's whore like my mother was. She was a drunk. She spent her life with men who were abusive. Most of the time, they abused me. My Aunt Bertie rescued me. Put me through school. Believed in me. That's why?"

"Not all men are like that Lucy." Duncan said soberly.

"Really, that is why even Sentry's famous power couple, Milo and Sydney can't get it together. Milo is stepping out with her best friend. Think of how sad it is for Sydney to lose both Milo and Jake." Lucy stated matter-of-factly.

"I don't know why some men are stupid. Women can be that way too. I think you will find someone that will love you the way, you deserved to be loved. I just wished you would let me show you I can be a contender for your heart. I don't believe in cheating. It's not hard sweet Lucy to love someone and devote themselves to them for years. My grandparents were married for sixty-five of them." He explained.

If Duncan kept it up, he would sneak into her heart. Lucy sighed and looked back at the picture. Maybe he was right. But being that a self-confirmed ladies' man was giving her this spiel, she was not ready to hop on the love wagon, just yet.

"Could Kelsey be involved? Isn't her hair brown?" Lucy changed the subject quickly.

"It could be." Duncan looked over her shoulder closer to the computer. "Lucy that is the woman we saw at the agency this morning. Look at her."

"Are you sure?" She squinted and looked closer.

"Why would Kelsey be stealing files? Do you think Sydney put her up to it?" Duncan asked.

"No but the caller said that she holds all the town's secrets. Think about it. She has the files including what Milo and Sydney paid to adopt Jake. She can release those files and ruin his career. A woman scorned is dangerous. It all makes sense."

The front door opened and suddenly Lucy felt a coolness in the room. She listened carefully and waited to see if she heard anything. Someone was in her apartment and she was about to find out who it was. Grabbing a .22 caliber pistol from her desk drawer, she walked out of the stairwell. Quietly tiptoeing down the stairs Duncan was right behind her.

Lucy tried to pace her breathing. Something was not right. She got to the front door and placed her hand on the knob and turned it quietly. She wanted to surprise whoever was on the other side.

"What the hell!" A voice shouted at her and she saw a flash in the dim light. Duncan didn't think. He pulled her out of harm's way ready to take the bullet for her. Kirk stepped into the light.

"What the hell Lucy. Are you going to blow my brains out?" Kirk said breathlessly.

"What are you doing in my apartment?" Lucy asked angrily nursing a fresh cut on her forehead from when she hit the railing. Duncan crouched beside her putting pressure on the wound.

"I am sorry to startle you Lucy, are you alright? Arlene forgot her purse. I knocked, and no one answered. I heard voices in the office, and I thought I would be in and out before anyone noticed." Kirk took a step toward her and Lucy was seething.

"I locked up Kirk, how did you get in here?" Lucy demanded.

"I still have a key. I was afraid if something happened to you, I could get in. I know you don't have anyone in your life anymore with your Aunt Bertie gone." Kirk crouched beside her.

"Give me my key back. Now! Get out of my house before I shoot you." Lucy said wincing in pain. Duncan took the key from Kirk and walked him to the door. He didn't want a homicide on his hands.

"Are you okay? I'm sorry I pushed you down. I thought he had a gun." Duncan said helping her up from the floor.

"No, he is an ass! You just saved me from blowing his brains out." Lucy said.

"Let's get you in and tend to that cut. Fortunately, it looks like a small one." He led her to a dining room chair and went to the bathroom. He gathered fresh towels and found some bandages in the medicine cabinet. He walked over to where she was sitting and cleaned the cut with some antiseptic.

"Ouch!" She jerked back from the cold.

"Hold still Tiger I will fix this in a minute." She shifted nervously in the chair with him so close. He worked quickly placing a bandage on the cut. "I think you're done now."

"Thank you." She spoke.

"You are most welcome. It was nice to save a man's life. The city might need Kirk tomorrow." He teased her lightly.

"He is so stupid sometimes, and he never treats me as an equal. It was the reason I quit being his partner. He used to get mad and refuse to sleep in the same room when I would outshoot him at the range." Lucy smiled wickedly remembering her fond memory.

"He was indeed a fool to leave your bed. I have only had a small taste and want so much more." He responded seductively stroking her cheek.

"I am going back to my office. I think I will call and check on Jenna. I want to make sure they are doing alright." She walked up the stairs to the solace of her office.

When Lila picked up, she was glad. She promised they would all stay out of harm's way. There was no one who knew where their location was, and it was going to stay that way.

When she hung up the phone, she looked over at Duncan. He was staring at her softly.

"I have a problem now. This woman who blew up my car wants me to bring Jenna and her baby to the park tomorrow night. If not, she will kill us both. Do you have any ideas?" She asked Duncan.

"Maybe we should tell Kirk." Duncan said.

"I am not sure that is a great idea. I have a feeling that it would be too hard for him to be biased. Milo is his best friend. You heard him say that he doesn't want to accuse anyone else of Melinda and Early's death. He believes Early killed Melinda. Suicide is no longer even on the table." Lucy sighed deeply and looked through the file on her desk. "I have no other choice but to find out for sure. I am calling Kirk and setting up that appointment with Kelsey. I need to get into her head."

"Let me go with you. I don't think it's safe to go alone. She could kill you." Duncan said.

"I can take care of myself, but you can tag along." She said carefully, not wanting to make him feel inferior to her. "You are the only one I can trust right now. I think that perhaps she might be a good suspect in both murders." Lucy said with a reasoning tone to her voice.

Chapter 23

Lucy woke up next to Duncan on the sofa. She looked down to make sure she was still dressed. She wriggled carefully out of his embrace. Looking at him sleeping, was almost calming. His eyes were closed, and he had a small peaceful smile pulling at the corners of his mouth. She wanted to just kiss him. She reached out and dabbed his face. He stirred a small bit. She was glad to wake up next to him. He demanded to stay close to her last night, and she really didn't mind so much.

They must've fell asleep while watching her favorite sci-fi flick. The Creature from Beyond was on one of the late shows. She remembered when she was with Kirk, he would never just be there to hold her. It was all sex and out the door.

"Boy, I was lucky to miss that life." She whispered under her breath.

"Lucky to miss what?" Duncan asked with a yawn.

"Nothing much. Just some thoughts rolling around in my head." She said.

He took her arm and pulled her back down.

"Sweet Lucy, you are still so beautiful." He whispered.

She laid her head on his chest. She could hear his heart beating.

"Duncan please don't say those things." She pleaded softly.

"Why? I am falling in love with you." He said as he kissed her hungrily.

She shot up from the sofa. "I demand that you don't fall in love with me."

"Don't deny you feel it too." He spoke. "But have it your way. I give up. There comes a time sweetheart when you are going to have to let someone in. If not me I hope someone. Because if not you will end up being old and lonely." He shouted.

"Grow up! When you find out what I am really like you will run away kicking and screaming. Just ask Kirk did. The only good thing this time is you won't have my best friend to screw on the way out." She said as anger and hurt flashed in her eyes.

"No, you're right there. I am not into cats. I somehow think that when you get older you will be holed up with thirty cats wondering if you regret your life." He argued.

"Go to hell!" She said as she slammed the door behind her.

"Gladly!" He countered behind a wall of loneliness.

Lucy needed air; the walls were closing in on her. She walked out the door. He was right Aunt Bertie was all she had when Kirk left. Then as fate would have it, she even left her. Kirk made her unsure of herself and these piddly little 'oh poor me!' you pushed me away games were going to stop. Lucy was angry and cynical. She was tired of Kirk constantly reminding her of how she was flawed. He didn't have to cheat on her. She would've given him her life. Just not marriage.

She found herself in front of Kirk and Arlene's apartment. Pulling the cell phone from her pocket, she called, and Arlene put her straight through with little thought this time. Thanks to Duncan for taking away her fears of stealing the idiot back.

"Kirk, I need to see you Colter's Park ten minutes." She hung up and went to the park to wait. If he had the right to demand that she drop everything for meetings and inserting himself into her life. Then hell, she could too. Lucy saw Kirk show up in a blue sweat suit. She waved him over.

"You don't look so good Lucy. What's wrong?" Kirk asked with concern.

"What was wrong with me? Why did you have to take up with my best friend Arlene? Was I really that bad to live with?" Lucy fought back tears.

"I am not doing this with you. God, Lucy it has been a year. Move on!" He said.

"No, you keep trying to pull me back in. I never got an explanation and if you still have any feelings left at all, you will talk to me. I turned inward destroying myself. So, I need to hear why? Just be honest." She said.

"Fine it was me. I was not man enough for you. You were competition at work, and everything was always about how tough Lucy was. I lived in your damn shadow for ten years. I was happy too because I loved you. However, I was not good enough for you." He said.

"I just said no! I never wanted you to leave or anything to change. I just said no." Lucy swiped tears off her cheek.

"You pushed me away when your Aunt Bertie was dying. Then you said no when I proposed. I just couldn't do it anymore. I didn't know how. I needed to be with someone who wanted me. I never meant to hurt you, honestly." He said with concern and care in his voice. She could see the hopelessness dashed from his eyes. She took a deep cleansing breath. He was right she didn't really want him.

"I am sorry about last night. I didn't mean to threaten to shoot you." She grinned lightly.

"I probably deserved it. You are a hard woman to stay away from Lucy. I fight the mistakes I made every day. I love Arlene, but I never meant to make you feel inferior. Arlene makes me feel like a protector. I was always too weak around you. I am sorry. Why do you think I kept your key? It was because I do still care. Duncan is one lucky bastard. I can tell you love him as much as he loves you." Kirk sighed deeply.

"I think I might have driven him away. It seems I have that effect on men." Lucy said.

She decided now was the time to change the subject. "I want to talk to Kelsey; can I have her number? I want to meet her." Kirk opened his phone and typed it into hers.

Kirk stood up and smiled warmly. "I need to go. Call Arlene she misses you. Again, we are sorry."

Lucy stayed seated on the bench. Shit happens in life. This was a very productive talk with Kirk. He was not right for her. Not because she was weak or flawed but because he couldn't handle her because she was too strong. Aunt Bertie was right.

The thought made her giggle. It was almost elating to hear herself laugh. She went home hoping to find Duncan. She owed him a huge apology. He was nowhere to be found. Her heart was sinking. She found a note on the table. She smiled lightly. He went for doughnuts and something about a peace offering. She heard a knock on the door.

Opening the door, she stood in amazement. There he stood with a white paper bag and flowers.

"I will win you over." He grinned sheepishly.

"Why knock? You practically live here these days." She spoke.

"Lucy, we need to talk. I need to tell you something." She moved from the doorway to the sofa.

"Alright." She said.

"I realized with all the little games of seduction we have been playing, you might have the wrong idea of me. I don't just do this with any woman. My past is over, and I don't take relationships lightly. I meant what I said earlier. I love you. I am sorry about the cat remark." He spoke.

"I love you too." She said.

"You do?" He whispered.

He wanted to pull her into him and hold her forever.

Lucy looked into his stunning green eyes trying to fight back tears. She really felt vulnerable at this moment. All cards were on the table, it scared her to express her feelings, but standing in front of him made her bold.

"Isn't it easy to see? I have been fighting so long to keep you at bay. I didn't want to drive you away. People have left me my entire life and when I realized I loved you. I couldn't breathe. I had a panic attack." Duncan pulled her close to him.

"Sweet Lucy, I will never walk away. You are my everything." She welcomed a long warm kiss. She stepped away from his embrace. It was time for her to lighten the moment.

"I want to get a better look at that wrestler body of yours, but it has to wait. I have to go and keep us from getting killed." She teased.

Chapter 24

She stepped out into the warm afternoon sun. Her heart was light and happy, but now the sudden thought of Kelsey, possibly ruining that was weighing heavily on her mind. Duncan eased her into the car with a warm hand on her back. They headed for the arranged meeting with Kelsey. The good thing was the little diner was wrapping up their lunch crowd.

"Are you nervous?" She asked, breaking the silence in the car.

"I will not lie. If she killed Melinda and Early that makes her able to hurt you. I am not sure I like you going alone to talk to her. It seems a little risky." Duncan turned the corner to the parking lot of Dipsy's Diner.

"I will be alright. Just sit tight. I will be back and if I need you, I will call you. Just keep a lookout here for me." Lucy leaned over and kissed him on the lips softly.

"Just be careful, my sweet Lucy." He said as she shut the car door.

Dipsy's Diner was quite a place. Located on the main street right outside of town, it fed many travelers and locals alike. The hostess stood behind a hot pink podium with a pencil cocked behind her ear.

"Can I help you?" She said with a winning smile.

"Kelsey Taylor please." Lucy looked around the room for the woman.

"Right this way, ma'am." She followed the hostess through the maze of tables to the right one.

Lucy could tell that Kelsey had a look of sadness upon her face. She looked at the woman and extended her hand politely.

"My name is Lucy." Kelsey motioned her to sit down.

"What did you need from me, Lucy? Milo said it was important that I talk to you." She sighed.

"Milo asked me to come to you and find out if you were a threat to his campaign. I know it is none of my business. I even hate coming to you like this, but Milo and Kirk thought you might need a female ear that wasn't involved in the situation. I know this must be hard for you." Lucy took a sip of water from her glass.

She could see that Kelsey was visibly shaken. She reached over and placed a comforting hand on hers.

"I love Milo. I didn't want to fall in love with him. It just happened. every day, I would watch Sydney rip him apart. It wasn't his fault that Jake died." Kelsey hiccupped with a high pitch voice. They paused their conversation while the server took their salad orders.

"I know how you feel. I was in the same situation with Kirk, but only in reverse. I was Arlene's best friend. I beat myself up for a long time. I guess that was the reason I felt compelled to meet you. I didn't want anyone else to go through what I did." Lucy said. "I think you just need to realize that you are much better than he is, and you are more worthy than being with a man that is not really yours."

"But I'm really not. I have done everything he has asked me to do. He still chose her." Kelsey wiped her eyes again and picked at her salad. "Sydney has forgiven me. I am just not sure I can forgive myself." Kelsey said sadly.

"There will come a time where you will forgive yourself and them. It just takes time." Lucy didn't know what else to say.

The two women sat in silence and ate their salads. She made a little small talk but in her head, she was thinking that Milo was an old dog.

Kelsey said her goodbyes and headed for her car. Lucy paid the check and ordered Duncan a Turkey and swiss on Rye. She waited for her order and tipped the server. She walked over to the door and opened it slowly. Duncan stirred from a catnap.

"Here's lunch." She handed him the takeout bag.

"Thanks, I'm starving. What did you find out?" Duncan took a bite of his sandwich.

"The woman was a basket case. I am not sure that she would have the guts to kill Early or Melinda. She was too busy grieving over the loss of Milo. Homicidal tendencies are not until later. Believe me, I know." Lucy said.

"Well, who could have done this? Could it have been Sydney?" Duncan asked.

"See, things are not adding up. I was hoping to get some clarity on the situation by now. I am still just as confused as I was before I arrived. Kelsey said that she did everything that Milo asked of her." Lucy sighed, here was the mystery of a lifetime laying right at her feet. Excitement and intrigue were what she dreamed about with her business, and now she just wished it were all over with.

Duncan pulled over into the parking lot of the office. She put her head back on the edge of the seat and peered over at him. It was a quiet, peaceful moment. She sighed and stepped out of the car, and they both went in silence to the office.

"Do you think Milo is a mastermind? I mean, think about it. Two women, both in love, eager to carry out a devious plan for murder. Maybe Kelsey wants to please him. Sydney has a mental breakdown. Maybe he orchestrated getting rid of Melinda for revenge." Lucy ran with her ideas as she sat down in her office chair behind her desk.

"What about Early? This person is interested in kidnapping Andrew. How can you connect the two?" Duncan was right. It was like there were two different crimes not connected. She shook her head in confusion.

"Unless he was in the wrong place and the killer saw him. Then they would need to silence him. Then Early said something about Sydney before he died. Maybe there is somebody in the picture that we are missing."

"He was dying and maybe confused. I think that whoever did this will be here tonight expecting to see Jenna and Andrew. How are we going to pull that off when all the likely suspects know who you are?" Duncan asked curiously.

"We have no other choice. We have to get Jenna back here. I will have to wire her and make the exchange with a doll. Maybe I can overtake her captor before she gets her hands on Jenna and find out who it is. If it is Kelsey or Sydney, I am sure I can take either of them in a fight." Lucy said.

"Should we talk to Kirk and see if he can lend his help?" Duncan asked carefully.

"I really don't want to. I have a feeling that Kirk would just say that my theories were nothing more than just bogus fiction. I can handle the situation. I have to before any more lives are hurt." She reasoned. "Besides, at this point we have more information on Melinda and everyone in town than the police do.

We have a bargaining chip of our own. We have those missing files." Lucy spun around in her desk chair, catching her notes off the short file cabinet behind her. Duncan walked over to her and leaned against her desk. His knees touched hers in a sweet fashion.

"You will be careful, sweet Lucy. If I lost you now, I don't think I could live." He traced a finger behind her ear to her collar, catching the wayward curl in the way. He placed a long and tender kisses on her lips.

"I promise. But I will need your help. I need some protection. I could use your lethal body to help me if things get out of hand tonight. I might need a strong arm." She licked her lips.

"My body is all yours in whatever capacity you need it, sweet Lucy."

"Lucy found the number for Jenna. Explaining the situation to Lila, Carol and Jenna who were listening on speaker phone. She tried to hide the fear in her voice.

They agreed to pack up and come back to the office. Lucy agreed to escort Jenna with a wired baby doll to the park. Then if the apprehension went well, all this will be over with quickly. If not, she would advise Jenna to start a new life elsewhere.

The cell phone chimed, and she looked at the number. She wondered what Kirk wanted.

"What's up?" She said. "Are you frigging kidding me? Thanks." Lucy's eyes were as large as saucers when she hung up the phone.

"What's wrong, Lucy?" Duncan asked.

"You will not believe this, but Melinda Hartgrove's body is missing from the morgue." Lucy said as she steadied herself against her desk.

"How can that be? A dead body just doesn't disappear." Duncan said curiously.

"This is becoming a nightmare. Every time I think this case is close to being solved, something else crazy happens. Jenna is on her way tonight to help us catch this person who is tormenting everyone. The only problem is we have now a long list of suspects, who can we trust?" Lucy walked over to her window and peered out. In just a few brief hours, she will have solved the biggest mystery in town. Who killed Melinda Hartgrove and Early Carter and why?

Chapter 25

Jenna stood there nervously as Lucy began wiring her up. She looked up at the young mother and realized she was terrified. She wished she could use a ringer to do the work, but everyone was now out in the open. No identity was hidden.

"Is all this really necessary?" Jenna said.

"I want to keep ears on you at all times. This is going to record our conversation so I can turn it over to the police. Jenna don't be a hero. Just waver on the side of caution. I am sending Duncan with you and he will protect you." She finished with all the wiring and helped her get into a bulletproof vest.

"I want to catch the person who wants to steal my baby and killed my husband. I will listen to you and Duncan." Jenna said with a newfound sense of bravery.

"I want you to wrap this doll up. Just like you would wrap up Andrew. Keep his face covered and hold him close to you." Lucy said. When she was done the phone rang right at a quarter till midnight. The park where the drop off was about to happen was less than five minutes away.

"Listen to me. Have Jenna bring the baby and sit on the third bench from the right. No police." The voice said.

"I will not let her do this unless she is escorted by an unarmed bodyguard. I want my girl protected." Lucy said carefully.

"Fine. I have a gun and I won't be afraid to use it if he tries anything. I will kill her if I need to. You have until midnight." The line went silent.

Lucy watched as Jenna went over and hugged Lila and Carol. She placed a light kiss on Andrew's forehead. Duncan swung into action and walked Jenna to the door and helped her into the car. Lucy slid into the front seat and turned to Jenna in the backseat.

"Buckle the doll in the car seat just in case we are being watched. It is dark and no one will tell." Lucy turned to Duncan and sighed nervously. He grabbed her hand to help calm her.

"Alright, we have the baby on board. We're off to kick some butt." Lucy was worried something would go terribly wrong. So many scenarios were still playing out in her mind. She wished she could just rewind the last several days and start all over again.

When Duncan arrived at the park, he watched Jenna carefully. He was keeping her directly in front of him so that no one would attack her from behind.

"Jenna, I am in your ear still. Just try to stay calm. I am going to get in a better position." Lucy went through the trees, taking cover near the third bench. She was dressed in camouflage gear and could not be seen against the backdrop of the trees at night. She held her position there for a few minutes.

A few feet away, she heard leaves crunching. She laid back a bit to see if she could make out where the noise was coming from. A thin figure came out of the woods. The woman settled behind Jenna. Duncan stood up and looked at the woman dressed in black. His eyes glazed over in surprise and she could tell that something was wrong.

"Melinda?" He said nervously as if he had seen a ghost.

"Duncan, so nice to see you, darling." She said lightly.

"What the hell? You were dead." He spoke.

"Only a minor hiccup in my plans. I knew you were too weak and spineless to help me. I had to do the only thing I could. I faked my death. Jenna had ruined everything. I could never cover my alibi for the Celia Barlow murder. Early came in and caught me on the phone masterminding my plan with Skip the pharmacy tech. He happened to overhear me talking about pinning the murders on Sydney. Damn, the boy tried to extort more money from me. So, I killed him." Lucy watched carefully, waiting for her to move. Melinda turned her gun on Jenna.

"Poor sweet Jenna. It's time for you to go be with your husband. I need that baby of yours." Melinda said calmly.

"Have you lost your ever-loving mind, Melinda?" Duncan shook his head nervously.

"I am indeed happy to see you. I wanted to know what it would be like to have my hands on your muscular body. Then you picked the P.I. over me." She hissed. "It was so nice toying with your new girlfriend. She is quite cute." Melinda kept her gun trained on Jenna.

"Melinda, you are insane." Duncan said.

Lucy stepped out from the shadows. She tackled Melinda to the ground. Duncan turned around when he heard a shot explode in the air. She and Melinda tumbled around as Duncan hurried Jenna back to the car to call the police. Duncan went quickly to where Melinda was choking Lucy and yanked her off. Lucy pulled herself up and gasped for air.

Melinda was fighting like a cat in the bathtub. It took everything that he could muster to hang on to her writhing body. Duncan reached around her and try to catch her in a bear hug. She took a bite out of Duncan's arm and he lost his grip.

"Son of a Bitch!" Duncan shouted in pain. She grabbed a gun that was stashed at her back and leveled it at Lucy.

"Okay, now here is the problem, Duncan. I have no problem killing your little girlfriend here." Flashing lights filled up the park. Lucy watched Melinda carefully. She could see that Kirk was approaching out of the corner of her eye. She felt his presence.

"Drop your weapon, Hartgrove." Kirk demanded.

"See now I can't do that." Melinda crowed again, acting as if nothing happened.

"Melinda, look, just put the gun down. I want to just talk." Kirk tried to reason with her.

"I am through talking." Melinda pulled the trigger, and a shot sailed through the air. Lucy spun, catching the bullet in her shoulder, and knocking the gun from her hand. She felt dizzy and passed out. Duncan saw red and anger took over. He penned Melinda to the ground and fought the gun away from her.

Kirk cuffed her and took Melinda to the squad car. The paramedics rushed over to Lucy to check out her wound. Duncan held her hand. When she came to, all she could see was the worry in his eyes. She squeezed his hand, trying to relieve his fears. The paramedics pulled her away from him and loaded her into the ambulance for a trip to the hospital.

"Hey man, are you alright?" Kirk asked Duncan who was trying to calm himself down.

"I am alright. She took a pretty sizeable chunk out of my arm." Duncan said.

"Reminds me of the time you bounced Bobby C out of Club Diesel." Duncan grinned and patted Kirk on the back.

"Good times. Thanks for standing by. I am glad you understood when I called this afternoon. She needed to do this on her own. Her confidence had been stripped. She just needed to get her confidence back in order. You really did a number on her man." Duncan said.

"I know and never meant to do that to her. I only wanted to take care of her. It just seemed like no matter how hard I pushed, she pushed back twice as hard. It was never meant to be. She never looked at me the way she looks at you. She is a force to be reckoned with. Let's go to the hospital and check on her. You need to get that bite looked at. You might need a rabies shot." Kirk teased lightly.

"I need to drop Jenna off at Lucy's before I go. Her mother is there with the baby." Duncan wished he could go to her and make sure she was going to be alright. Of course, his Lucy was tough, and she could take care of herself.

Kirk summoned an officer to take Jenna home. He wanted to make sure that Duncan made it to the hospital.

KIRK WALKED INTO THE emergency room. Lucy shifted in her bed, trying to get comfortable. He smiled at her as he walked in.

"How is Duncan? Did Jenna get back alright?" Lucy asked.

"Duncan is having his bite treated. Melinda took a good chunk out of his arm. I made sure Jenna got home safely." He said.

"He called you, didn't he?" Lucy cocked an eyebrow at him.

"Only because he wanted to make sure you were safe. He made a deal with me. I told him I would stand down until you made your capture or needed me." Kirk explained.

Lucy rolled her eyes. She didn't know whether to be hurt or grateful he went behind her back. She looked over at Kirk who was trying to read her thoughts.

"Thank you for coming. I never could've taken her down by myself." She said.

"Lucy, we always made excellent partners. We just were lousy lovers. I always have your back. I want to be friends." Kirk took her hand gently.

"That would be good." Lucy said earnestly.

"I also asked Duncan to come be my assistant. He is coming on to work for me in the offices. The boy needs some way to support himself." Kirk said.

"He is a great man. Very smart. Duncan would be a great asset to the department." Lucy said. "One other thing, I have all of Melinda's private records. I hope Milo doesn't take the heat on Jake's adoption. I have to turn the records over to the feds." Lucy reasoned with Kirk.

"Do the right thing, I will give Milo a heads up. They can have their attorney on hand, should they need one. Kelsey turned over the missing files. Seems like she is not out to destroy Milo after all." Kirk said.

Duncan came into the room. Kirk looked at the sling on his arm.

"Well, do you get to keep your arm?" Kirk teased.

"Yeah, I think the sling is a bit overkill, but the nurse insisted. I told her I needed to check on my kick-butt princess." Duncan kissed Lucy on the forehead.

"How is the shoulder sweet Lucy?" He grazed a quick kiss on her lips.

"Hurts like hell, but I can go home soon." She said.

Chapter 26

Jenna smiled when Lila and Carol came in with Andrew. Are you through with me for the day, Lucy? I want to take Andrew to the park." Lucy looked up from her newest case file. Jenna was becoming a real asset to have around. In the last two weeks she had been a great help to her. Jenna was turning her life around. She hired Jenna full time to help her in the office.

"Have fun. I need to go get ready for my date, anyway." Lucy lost track of the time.

Lila and Carol spent every bit of extra time with Andrew. It thrilled Lucy with the way their lives had turned out. She still thought of Early often and wished she could have saved him, but at least now his death was not in vain.

Melinda Hartgrove was locked up tight behind bars awaiting trial. There was no way with all the murder and mayhem she had caused that she would get less than a lifetime sentence.

Lucy couldn't believe she would not be home eating Chinese food with Jinx. She got her sling removed, and the wound was healing nicely. Her life was finally back on course and it was great.

She walked into her apartment and stepped into the shower. She was running late. Getting out and applying her make-up, she felt happy and confident again for the first time in a long while. She pulled out a super sexy red dress. It had thin straps and a daring slit up the side. When she saw it, she knew Duncan would love it.

It was crazy the deal they made to one another, but somehow it strangely worked. Duncan wanted time to get started on his new job and make some new plans. He called her and they would spend hours talking nightly. She found out he used to be a bouncer for some of the wildest clubs in town before he worked for Melinda. She loved the phone conversations, but at the end of them, she longed for his touch.

Finally, tonight, after four weeks of being physically apart, they had their first official date, and she was excited. She put her high-heeled sandals on and put a spritz of perfume on her wrists and neck. She grabbed a lace shawl from the closet and left the house.

When she arrived at Cooper's Place, the crowd was buzzing. She walked up to the bar.

"Hey Paul, have you seen my man?" She asked while sitting on a bar stool.

"Wow, Lucy, you look amazing. I bet that man of yours will be thrilled to see you." Paul said while giving her a beer.

"He sure will." Kirk said as he kissed her on the cheek. "The Duncanator will be here soon. He had to finish up some paperwork. I hope he doesn't have a heart attack with you in that dress. Should I keep the paramedics on standby?" Kirk teased.

"I am sure we will be fine." She smirked.

"Hello, gorgeous." A male voice caught her attention. "I rarely do this, but I am going to sit beside you while you wait for your date. Has anyone ever told you how stunning you are? I will keep those guys over there from bothering you." He leaned in intimately, closing the gap between them.

"That has to be the cheesiest pickup line I have ever heard. Does that actually work with women?" She grinned seductively.

"I am hoping it works with you and me." Duncan wrinkled his nose with a playful grin on his lips.

"Your place or mine." She said confidently.

"I have Rocky Road and Black Forest cake. I would love to show you how to eat them properly. I also would love to get a look of that dress a little closer." He winked at her as he ran his finger up her leg to the top of the slit in her dress.

"Definitely your place then." She leaned into him and caught his lower lip between hers.

When he escorted her out of the bar, she was excited. His hand was placed possessively on the small of her back.

When they arrived at his apartment, she smiled. The table was set with Black Forest cake as promised. She now had her cake, and she would enjoy it later. She had other things on her mind now. A wicked grin crossed his lips, and she could feel her body surge with desire. She did the only thing a girl could do in her situation. She threw her arms lovingly around his neck.

"Tonight, I am all yours. I love you, Duncan." She said breathlessly.

"I love you too my sweet Lucy." He removed the Clark Kent glasses and scooped her up. He carried her into his bedroom determined to show her he indeed was her superman. The night belonged to them. She couldn't wait to love him for the rest of her life.

About the Author

Stacey Watts loves telling stories, as her writing reflects this. She currently lives in a small town in Texas with her husband and three children. Her imaginative spirit will not disappoint as she weaves stories of romance and intrigue. An author with Self-Published works; she invites you to consider her words.